The
Circle
of
Life

The
Circle
of
Life

SUDHA
MURTY

PENGUIN BOOKS

An imprint of Penguin Random House

PENGUIN BOOKS

Penguin Books is an imprint of the Penguin Random House group of companies
whose addresses can be found at global.penguinrandomhouse.com

Published by Penguin Random House India Pvt. Ltd
4th Floor, Capital Tower 1, MG Road,
Gurugram 122 002, Haryana, India

First published in Penguin Books by Penguin Random House India 2025

10 9 8 7 6 5 4 3 2 1

This book is a work of non-fiction. The views and opinions expressed in the book
are those of the author only and do not reflect or represent the views and opinions
held by any other person.

Please note that no part of this book may be used or reproduced in any manner
for the purpose of training artificial intelligence technologies or systems.

ISBN 9780143474296

Typeset in Adobe Caslon Pro by Manipal Technologies Limited, Manipal
Printed at Replika Press Pvt. Ltd, India

www.penguin.co.in

Indian Institute of Science, Bangalore

To life,
which has shown me many colours,
plenty of ups and downs,
and taught me the invaluable lessons that
no book can teach

Author's Note

Life is a great leveller.

Life is also enchanting and unfolds its secrets in different ways.

I have chosen the Indian Institute of Science, popularly known as IISc or Tata Institute, a real setting for this fictional story about the life of five people. Their hardships, joys, achievements and failures have been woven into this tale that spans twenty-five years, from 1998 to 2023. I have chosen IISc on purpose because it is my alma mater. Every nook and corner of this place is familiar to me.

I want to thank Milee Ashwarya of Penguin Random House India and Shivani Khanwalkar of Murty Trust, who have helped bring this book out.

Monologue

Uttara

I am happy and scared; I am enthusiastic and worried. Today, I have two opposing emotions pulling me apart because it is the last week of July, and all my friends are coming for a reunion after twenty-five years. What a long gap it has been . . . So much water has flown under the bridge. So much has happened in two-and-a-half decades in my personal and professional life.

In 1999, all of us were worried about Y2K—potential computer errors related to the formatting of calendar dates after the year 2000. Today, we are talking about artificial intelligence. WhatsApp came to us only in 2015 but has made us completely dependent on it. Postcards have vanished. Telegrams have been buried. This meeting of ours was not an unexpected one; its date, time and venue were decided twenty-five years ago.

At that time, we were very young, probably twenty-four or twenty-five years old. We were so confident in our lives then, and now, as we meet, it remains to be seen what has happened to that confidence.

Though in my heart, I feel very happy that I will be meeting all my dear friends, I have an inferiority complex, because I am not successful like them. I feel sad. All my friends are thriving. That said, meeting such people is always a joy.

My friend, to whom I would lend my saris for any good occasion once upon a time, today received the highest award she could in her career.

The man who was shy of his poverty has now become a rich person. The person who was penniless, and whom I nursed in my house like my brother, has become the industry minister in the Centre. The woman, who had clarity of thought in moments when all of us were confused, has become a tech entrepreneur in America. Twenty-five years ago, all of them were unknown people. Today, because of their hard work and relentless pursuit of their career, they are all well off. Compared to them, when I look at myself in the mirror, what I can see are a few grey hairs and an ordinary life.

Uttara Rao sighed and got up from the chair and went towards the kitchen.

1999

It was the end of July, and dark clouds had covered the sky. It seemed as if it would pour down any moment. Bangalore used to be a hill station, but not anymore. It has become a cement jungle and has turned warmer; a slight cold wave could still be experienced in July.

However, students gathered at the main building of the Indian Institute of Science (IISc) were not bothered about the weather. They were very happy and had lots of enthusiasm on their faces. Some of them felt they had won the war of academics.

The red sloping roof of the main entrance building stood prominently on the campus. Students who had come there were looking at each other as if they were each other's competitors. To get into IISc was not easy. They had to clear examinations, run the hurdles, and swim the sea of knowledge to emerge like champions.

Getting a gold medal, distinction or a rank is extremely common in IISc though it may be considered tough and a great achievement elsewhere. There is a saying that women in Malaya Mountain use sandalwood to cook since it grows there. Similar is the case with IISc, where intelligence is a common factor among everybody. If you are bright, IISc makes you brighter. If you are a researcher, the Institute makes you a scholar. It is the seat of learning that polishes your knowledge.

Opposite the main building is a statue of Jamsetji Tata holding the prototype of the Institute in his hand and smiling. Happiness reflects on the statue's face. Very few people know that he had given away one-third of his property in 1896. At that time, the British Governor-General Robert Clive denied higher education for Indians, thinking they were incapable of it. But Jamsetji took up the challenge and Krishnaraja Wadiyar IV of Mysore Kingdom had given three hundred acres of land for free. It resulted in the Institute and so, top-class scientists were produced.

Everything is miniscule in front of knowledge. That is the rule of every institute. Aditya Varma, the son of great industrialist Vikram Varma, had flown from Delhi and was standing in the queue, waiting for his admission card.

Swaminathan, the gold medalist from IIT Chennai, the son of a schoolteacher, was behind him. Mary Kutty, the daughter of nurse Gracy from Kottayam, Kerala, who secured a first rank from her university, was next. Their financial positions did not matter. They were all students of IISc. The queue was moderate. Nobody knew who among those in the queue would become great scientists or technocrats; the world would bow down to them in a few years. But there was one thing common in all of them. They were all ambitious and knew what they had to prove and did not need any monitoring. They were self-reliant and self-motivated.

This is the story of five people: Uttara Rao, Janaki Paranjape, Arvind Shah, K. Subba Rao and Sumithra Iyer, who are currently hundreds of kilometres away from Bangalore, on their way to meet each other.

This story is of their success, failure, happiness and sadness at the hands of destiny.

Uttara
Rao

[
We are no other than a moving row,
Of magic shadow-shapes that come and go

—Omar Khayyam
]

Lakshmi Nivas was a prominent bungalow in the Banjara Hills of Hyderabad. It is a place where the rich and powerful people from Tollywood live. During the Nizam's time, Rama Rao was an engineer and had helped to construct different prominent buildings in Hyderabad. It was not very crowded those days, and the Nizam had liked his work and rewarded him with a big plot. Later, after Independence, his son Venkateshwara Rao started a company called S.V. Constructions and became a well-known engineer in Hyderabad. They were great devotees of Lord Venkateshwara of Tirupathi.

Venkateshwara Rao handled several government projects. He had three children. The eldest, Umesh, helped him with the constructions, though he did not have any formal qualification in civil engineering. Then there was Uttara, and the youngest was Shamala.

It was not very warm in the second week of July, but Uttara was still feeling hot. She was sitting on the steps of her house. Though the coolers were on, she was uncomfortable. Opposite her, her grandfather Rama Rao was sitting in an armchair with a newspaper, but his focus was on Uttara who was knitting a sweater. Uttara's siblings were playing tennis on the court adjacent to the house.

'Uttara, why are you knitting a sweater? Is it for you to take to Bangalore?' asked her grandfather.

Uttara smiled. 'It is not for me. It is for you.'

'Ha, what a joke! Having a sweater in Hyderabad is as good as selling refrigerators to Eskimos,' laughed Rama Rao.

The sun was setting, and its rays fell on Uttara's ear studs. The diamond earrings were a gift from Uttara's late grandmother. Rama Rao remembered his wife because Uttara resembled her very much. She had long hair, a slightly dark complexion and, more or less, was an introvert; but she was extremely intelligent. Uttara had completed her engineering degree from Osmania University and had done very well. She was a rare combination of wealth and knowledge.

Rama Rao had studied in IISc's civil engineering department more than sixty years ago, and more than three decades ago, his son Venkateshwara Rao had graduated from the same department. And now Uttara was about to join the Institute. However, she had applied to study computer science, unlike her father and grandfather.

Uttara's siblings were not as academically inclined. Rama Rao and his son felt that Uttara had to take their company forward, but she was unsure. She always felt running a company required a different skill set which she did not have.

Uttara suddenly remembered something, got up and went inside. She returned within five minutes and continued.

'What happened?' asked her grandpa.

Uttara smiled and said, 'Grandpa, I went in to check my email.'

'Regarding what?' Rama Rao was anxious.

'Regarding my admission to IISc.'

'What happened? I hope our tradition remains intact.'

'Relax Grandpa, I have got admission.'

'Oh! That is great news!' grandpa clapped and cheered.

Uttara did not show much enthusiasm and continued knitting.

Hearing the clap, Umesh and Shamala stopped their game and came running. 'What is the big news, Grandpa? You are clapping!' said Umesh.

'Yes, we should celebrate. Uttara got admitted to IISc.'

'Oh,' they said and did not bother much.

'That means Uttara is going to Bangalore?' asked Shamala.

Umesh reminded, 'You remember that we have dinner at Raj Bhavan, right?'

'Yes, but I am not coming,' said Uttara.

'I expected that.'

'I want to spend time with Grandpa.'

Her brother and sister went inside to get ready.

'Where are your parents?' asked Rama Rao, eager to share the joy that he was unable to contain.

Her mother had gone to a fashion show, and her father was busy with some government delegates.

Rama Rao was disappointed. He knew his daughter-in-law Kamakshi was into jewellery and fashion. She still thought that she was very young and would often forget that she had a twenty-three-year-old daughter. Kamakshi performed puja and other festivals—not out of devotion, but simply to show off and compete with other elite families in Banjara Hills.

The grandeur of each festival increased year after year, though devoid of faith. Rama Rao was sad for a minute but cheered up when he looked at Uttara. She was unlike her mother. Instead, she was simple, loving, knowledgeable and very sincere.

He looked at her and said, 'Uttara, I am not sure if I will be around but when you have children, please see that they also join IISc. Our family tradition should go on.'

'Grandpa, where will you go? I will return to Hyderabad after my studies and will be here with you. You will see us every day,' Uttara replied to lighten up Rama Rao's mood.

As she completed the sweater, Uttara got up. No one knew her destiny; she may never return to Hyderabad after some years.

K. Subba Rao

[
Arthathuranam na gurur na bandhu . . .
Persons obsessed with becoming rich have
no friends and relatives.
]

It was a cold night. Subbu wanted another blanket, but he was aware that in their house each of them could have only one. Even in his dreams, he wished that his father had more money to buy extra rugs. His house was in a small lane near the Malleswaram railway station. It was a locality packed with several houses, and everyone knew everyone else in the vicinity. His father, Rajanna, was a postman, and he had three children—Subbu, Mangala and Diwakar. He had been living here ever since he married Gowramma and brought her in. Both knew that it was hard for them to move out of their rented house. Children were growing up and so were the expenses. Of all his children, Subbu was the most hardworking and intelligent. He completed his education from the tenth standard onwards on scholarship money. Rajanna and Gowramma were indeed proud of his achievements and looked at him as their future with hope.

He graduated from Visvesvaraya College of Engineering, popularly known as UVCE, a coveted institute in Bangalore. To be able to study there with a scholarship and pass with distinction, was like an icing on the cake. He knew his father's difficulties and hence, had never requested any extra money other than what they would give. He would occasionally give home tuition and earn the amount required to buy books or stationery. Whenever he visited the homes for tuition, he would feel how lucky his students were to live in a big house, enjoy the comforts and roam around in chauffeur-driven cars. This deepened his desire to do well in life and enjoy a similar lifestyle one day.

He made up his mind to study well, work hard and become rich, come what may.

Rajanna and Gowramma celebrated their son's success in their own small way—sharing the news with all neighbours and friends and distributing sweets.

Rajanna wanted him to take up a job in Bangalore, instead of studying further. *There are many good companies in Bangalore*, he thought. *Though he is a mechanical engineer, he is good at computers. He will easily get a software job at Infosys, Wipro or TCS. They are all here, in Bangalore. He can get a good salary and that can reduce my burden. He will easily get a good alliance with any engineer girl. They both can settle down comfortably. After working for four or five years, he can go abroad. Skilled employees are often sent abroad. His life will be very good.* But he could not tell this to his grown-up son. He felt shy to tell all of this to Subbu, to share the responsibility of the family. He only shared his opinion with Gowramma.

Gowramma thought differently. 'Let us ask him, we are not educated like him. He is intelligent and sensitive and understands the family situation. Let him decide.'

Subbu never talked about anything, nor did he share his ideas. He always planned and kept it to himself. He was sceptical that if they didn't turn out successful, then people would look down upon him.

The previous day, he had told his mother, 'Amma, I got admission to IISc. I want to study there.'

Gowramma was very happy to know that he wanted to go for higher studies. Rajanna felt offended that his son was neither taking up a job nor had he shared his plans with him.

'When had you applied?' he asked.

'A month ago, I took an entrance exam. I got the results only today.' He could read his father's face and continued. 'Appa, I will get a full scholarship. Don't worry.'

'Why did you not tell this before?' Rajanna probed further.

'If I had told you, it would have been as good as telling the neighbours. We can never discuss any private matters here. Immediately, every passerby will come to know. I didn't want that. We should shift from this place in the future. We will get our own independent apartment.'

Gowramma was very happy that her son was envisaging the things her husband could not.

'Subbu, may all your dreams come true. I know that you are capable and will surely achieve what you visualize. Let me prepare your favourite meal, kheer and bisi bele bath for today's lunch,' she said and went inside the kitchen.

Janaki
Paranjape

[
Though my child is crying and not allowing me
to do any household work, I still wish to have
many more children around me, even if the
household work lags.
]

Shreyas Apartment was known as a residential place for working professionals. It was located in Deccan Gymkhana, making it very convenient for middle-class people to move around the city. In their fourth-floor three-bedroom apartment, Janaki was sitting on the balcony and tightening her tennis racket. She was a good tennis player, clear-headed and very logical in her conversations. Her fair complexion and greenish eyes had made Janaki a darling among the apartment's residents—her personality was like a magnet.

Her parents were Dr Paranjape and Meera. Their marriage was a little unusual in those days. Meera was a widowed nurse in the same medical college where Dr Paranjape was working. Though Dr Paranjape was from a traditional orthodox family, he was influenced by Mahatma Karve. Karve himself had married a widow and advocated for their education. So, Dr Paranjape and Meera got married.

He stayed in Sadashiv Peth. His parents disliked Meera because she was a widow. So, he stepped outside his Maharashtrian family and crossed the

15

River Mula to the other side of the city into the Deccan Gymkhana vicinity. They had Janaki. She became their only child as Meera was unable to conceive again due to her ill health.

Janaki was called '*tayi*', meaning 'sister', in their building. She was like a Pied Piper for children, who would follow her everywhere. If any child was crying, their mother would come to Meera's house and give their child to Janaki.

A child without siblings could turn out to be self-centred, but Janaki was an exception. She would share everything with all the children in their building. Like any other child, when she was young, she wanted to become a teacher. Later, when she got a little older, she would say she wanted to be a doctor, and during her teens, she was interested in becoming a pilot. But once she completed her BSc and joined IISc for her engineering, all these immature wishes disappeared. She was fascinated to become a computer scientist and an entrepreneur.

Dr Paranjape felt very sad. He had his own nursing home and had a good clientele of patients, and now, he had to hand them over to some outsider.

But Meera was more accommodating. 'Don't be disappointed. Every generation disappoints the next generation, be it by not choosing the family profession or in some other way. Are we not the best example? Janaki is good in many fields. Let her do what she likes. We have given her freedom after BSc. Let her live happily—the way she wants.'

Her tennis coach suggested, 'Janaki, if you concentrate only on tennis, you will play at the national level. Think about it.'

'No, sir. I just enjoy playing this game as a hobby. My aim is different,' Janaki replied curtly and cut off his expectations.

Soon she went to Bangalore and completed her undergraduate degree from IISc. Now she had come to Pune for her holidays. She had applied for post-graduation from IISc and took the entrance exam. As she was bright and confident, she knew that she would certainly secure a seat for post-graduation.

The news was confirmed by email. Janaki went inside and started packing. Compared to others, her excitement was slightly less as she was already used to the campus for the last three years.

Meera sat on the sofa, thinking of Janaki. She knew her daughter would not return to Pune after her post-graduation. She would prefer to go abroad. Once young adults leave home, they rarely return. Meera looked out from the window. She saw a young bird flying into the sky.

Arvind
Shah

At the age of twenty, if you are not an idealist,
you don't have a heart.
At the age of forty, if you continue to be
an idealist, you don't have a brain.

—Unknown proverb

Arvind was called a rebel by his brothers. He was known to be impractical among his friends. But he was appreciated by his teachers. Yet his father, Chandmalji, would say, 'He is a motherless child, and life will teach him many lessons. And, after all, he is a kid.'

Everyone knew that Arvind was straightforward and bright. He despised traits such as hypocrisy, showing off or lying. He was fond of books, an introvert but extremely helpful to people and believed that the right people can shape the future. His sisters-in-law always blamed him behind his back. He was good to everybody but was considered a burden to the family. No one loved him unconditionally.

Seth Chandmalji was a well-known businessman in Kanpur. He started his life in poverty and rose to become a millionaire in the present day. He studied till the tenth grade but had a PhD in common sense—he could assess people, analyse risk and had excellent business acumen. With these skills, he had developed many businesses, a construction company, a mall, different types of shops, a warehouse etc. His first two

children, Ramesh and Suraj, were born in the early
years of his marriage, and as a family tradition, were
also married early. Both brothers were their father's
right hand. Much later in life, Shanti, Chandmalji's
wife, conceived again, and Arvind was born. Due
to her being middle-aged and other complications,
Shanti was doubtful if she would survive after the
delivery, and had taken a promise from her husband,
saying, 'I know you have two daughters-in-law, two
of your widowed sisters and many other people to
take care of in this house. But no one can replace a
mother. You should become both a mother and father
to this child.'

Chandmalji felt sorry that he was losing Shanti
and vowed that he would live up to her wish. Hence,
he was very lenient towards Arvind. He was raised
at home with all the women around but not attached
to anyone in particular. Suraj and Ramesh did not
complete their graduation but were good at business.
Chandmalji was disappointed but was happy that they
were mastering the tricks of the trade. However, he
yearned for at least Arvind to complete a degree. And
similarly, Arvind did exceedingly well in school and
got many awards. His father was happy about his
progress. Chandmalji would give gifts to everyone in
the house for each Diwali, but Arvind would always
ask for money instead. During one of the Diwalis, he
had bought an entire set of books for himself. Another
year, he donated all the money to an orphanage,
whereas other relatives purchased gold and silver.

Arvind always wore khadi clothes and remained in his own world. Chandmalji now stayed at home and had asked Ramesh and Suraj to take care of the business. Nobody bothered about what Arvind did. There was hardly anyone who paid attention to him, and gradually, he grew up as an idealist.

He would take cold water baths, sleep on the mat and never use any luxury items in his life.

When the board exam results were announced, Arvind had topped Kanpur city. The school called Chandmalji and told him, 'Your son is an ideal student. He is like a *rishi*. In olden days, rishis would go to the forest and do penance. Same way he will do penance for studies. He will bring a great name to you and your family.'

Chandmalji was very happy and wanted to share the joy with his older sons.

However, when he told his sons, they had a different opinion about Arvind. 'Baba, he is of no use. We should train him properly. Let him do B.Com. He can converse with higher authorities in English. Let him learn all the techniques to evade tax.'

Arvind, who was also a part of the conversation, was surprised by their opinion and revolted, 'I will neither cheat our government nor do B.Com. I don't have any interest in business. I will apply to IIT and if I get in, I will do engineering.'

'Getting into IIT is not that easy, people say. If you don't get into IIT, will you do B.Com?' asked his father.

'If I don't get into IIT, I will go to some other engineering college but definitely not do B.Com,' Arvind said and walked away.

Arvind applied to IIT and prepared for the exam without tuition. He got through and chose civil engineering. Initially, he would cycle from home to the IIT campus. Chandmalji would feel sad for he always used his Mercedes, and his other two sons drove their separate cars.

When he saw Arvind cycling, he remembered his wife, and it would hurt him. But Arvind would not listen. He was fond of his nephews and nieces, and so, he would spend his weekend with them.

After a month, he decided that he would not stay at home and said, 'Baba, I want to stay in a hostel.'

His father reasoned with him; he said that the food was not up to the mark in hostels. Still, Arvind did not bother. He took minimum luggage and left for the hostel.

Sometimes, he would come home and see the children.

He finished B.Tech with good marks and applied to IISc for master's. He awaited the results.

However, Chandmalji had a different idea. At his age, both his sons were married. Getting a good girl in the community was very difficult. *With Arvind's degree, he could get a wealthy alliance and settle down*, he thought. He wished for Arvind to take over their construction company. But Arvind disagreed with the idea of getting married and brushed aside his father's wish saying he had many better things to do in life.

His brothers also suggested that they should find a suitable girl and pressure him into marrying, and afterwards, she would take care of him, so they wouldn't be responsible for him anymore.

Chandmalji knew life better than them. 'No, we should not spoil the girl's life. This fellow will not listen to anyone. Not only will he not marry, but if we pressure him, he might go away from home. This should not be our headache. Let us see later.'

One day, Arvind wanted to talk to his father and went to their factory. But after reaching there, he found that Chandmalji had gone to Meerut for some work. Arvind sat down for some time to write notes when two factory inspectors came in. Arvind did not get up. That irritated the inspectors, but the old munshi came running, bowed down to them and invited them inside, 'Please come in, *sethji* has gone to Meerut.' Munshi was aware that they had come for their monthly ritual. Arvind was sitting near the cashbox.

Munshi knew that he had to pay them their usual cut, but how could he take the cash without telling Arvind? It would be unethical.

He requested Arvind, 'Beta, can I take twenty thousand from the cash box please?'

'Please take,' he said. Then he curiously asked, 'For what?'

Munshi softly whispered, 'I have to give it to the inspectors.'

Arvind was shocked. He said, 'Why should you give it to them?'

Munshi requested again, 'You don't worry, this is a practice.'

'If our product is good enough, they have to certify, not otherwise.'

Arvind held on to his point.

The two inspectors who were outside the cabin could hear the conversation, due to Arvind's raised voice. They yelled at the munshi, 'Munshiji, we are leaving . . .'

Munshi was in a dilemma. 'Beta, this is business. A little bit of plus and minus is normal.' Arvind was not moved. He got up and said, 'No, we will not do this. This amounts to corruption, and our country will never progress.' Arvind straightaway approached the inspectors and said, 'Please inspect; if our product is not good, we will improve it. When you come next time, it will be as per your standard. But we will not give you twenty thousand rupees.'

Listening to that, the inspectors' anger knew no bounds.

'Are you giving twenty thousand as a donation to us? Please realize that if I go as per the rules, we could find hundreds of errors in your factory. By law, with those errors, I can close the factory. If you think twenty thousand is a gift to us, your father should give a bigger gift to the minister. Otherwise, how will you run the business? If you want the report about your factory, please come to our office and collect it,' they huffed and left.

Arvind did not know what to do. By that time, the munshi had called Ramesh and Suraj. After half an hour, the brothers came and yelled at Arvind, 'You are a most impractical person. According to the statement that you made today, we will have to shell out fifty thousand and maybe more. Worse than that is that we must go and touch their feet.'

Without emotion, Arvind replied, 'Yes, when you make a bad product, when you keep the factory dirty, when you make bad cement, you have to pay for it. Many houses, which poor people build using your cement with their lifetime savings, will collapse . . .'

'My dear brother, you are very principled but keep it to yourself. Please don't ever interfere in our business. That will be of great help to us,' Ramesh said. Seeing no point in arguing further, they left.

When Chandmalji returned in the evening, there was a big *darbar*. Both sides accused each other, and the father understood both cases.

He realized what had transpired. The only way to save business was to send Arvind out of Kanpur and fortunately, on that day, he had received the news of his admission at IISc, Bangalore. So, that was a mutual relief to all of them.

When his idealist son would return after two years, Chandmalji would again have to worry about how to handle him.

Sumithra
Iyer

[
I slept and dreamt that life was beauty
I woke up and realized that life was duty

—Lord Byron
]

That year, the summer in Chennai was unbearable. Scorching heat and humidity made lives miserable. An evening walk on the beach brought solace, but for Sumithra, who came from an orthodox family, even this small respite was impossible.

Vaidyanathan, her father, was a schoolteacher and for two generations, he and his family had stayed in the same house in the same lane of the same city. Nothing had changed; the wind of modernity had never touched their house though it had breezed through other homes. Vaidyanathan's mother Seethamma and her sister Lakshmi Andal—who were supposed to go to their heavenly abode long back but did not by sheer luck—and his own sister Devamma, who was widowed at teenage, had created a fort of orthodoxy in their house. God had forgotten about Lakshmi Andal's presence in Chennai and instead had taken away her husband by accident.

These three women had extraordinary theories about life, horoscopes, blind beliefs and orthodoxy.

It seemed as if any fort could be conquered but this iron fortress in Vaidyanathan's house could not be touched.

Within this fort was the delicate, beautiful Sumithra, who could not break out, unless she could find Alladin's lamp.

Sumithra was very beautiful. She had curly dark locks, pretty eyes and deep dimples. She was good academically, a great cook, respected elders, hardworking and very active. She was seen as an ideal daughter-in-law for any family. But the three women would always say, 'Poor Vaidya, Sumi is a thorn in his life.'

Sumithra's parents did not have any say in their house, which was dominated by the three women.

In those days in any arranged marriage, horoscopes played an important role. She was considered doomed because of her horoscope, which said that she would be widowed very soon after the marriage. When Sumithra's horoscope was shared with a prospective groom, it would be returned saying that it did not match. There were very few families who did not believe in horoscope, and if they came for alliance, these three women would scare them on the pretext of being frank in their conversation. They would say, 'Please be careful. Sumithra has this defect in her horoscope.' Or Devamma would cry in front of them and say, 'My horoscope was not checked before I was married as we were related. Look at my state now.' So, no one was ready to marry Sumithra.

People who came with great disbelief in horoscope and astrology, would get scared of these women and leave.

Poor Sumithra would observe everything from the window of her room and shed tears in silence.

She had twin sisters who were ten years younger than her. Their wedding was a distant dream.

The only hope was that Sumithra would find a groom on her own, but that was next to impossible in Chennai. In her community, everyone knew about her horoscope. Sumithra never wanted to be in Chennai and wanted to get out of home and away from this choking atmosphere. So, she applied for a PhD in chemistry at IISc in Bangalore.

After her MSc, she started working with Prof. Keshavan as a research assistant.

'Sumithra, if you get a seat at IISc, you should go at any cost. Pursuing a PhD there will give you better international exposure. Afterall, IISc is the abode of knowledge,' he would say.

She went for the interview and did well. Sumithra hoped to get a seat, and maybe a ticket for her future with it. While in the lab, she got a rejection letter for her PhD. She went to her room quietly and started crying. Every drop of tear from her eyes indicated her failure. The door of the dam had opened and with it, her fears flooded out—failing to get a groom or not getting admission meant that she had to stay in the same house.

Tears rolled down for long. Prof. Keshavan, who had come to pick up some books, saw her sad face and consoled, 'Sumithra, don't cry. This is not the end of life. You can pursue a PhD in Chennai and do well in life. Many people have done that. Ultimately, it is not any institute, but you who will make it.'

Hearing these kind words, Sumithra wiped her tears and washed her face.

'Yes sir, I will work hard and not disappoint you. Can I come at 7 a.m.?'

Keshavan nodded. He told himself, 'She is such a good student. Probably she might have got scared at the interview. She is also shy. Anyway, it is their loss and my advantage.'

Little did he know that along with Sumithra, he also would move to IISc some day.

This is the story of three women, Sumithra Iyer, Uttara Rao, Janaki Paranjape, and two men, Arvind Shah and Subba Rao.

They all came from varied strata of society—from different states and communities, and spoke different languages. But there was one thing in common: their love for knowledge. For that sake, they were all set to leave their homes and familiar environments and arrive at Bangalore to fulfil their ambition.

Their struggle for life is the story of this book.

Uttara was packing her suitcase when Kamakshi, her mother, came with another, full of silk saris and ornaments. Uttara kept it aside and Kamakshi was upset. 'We have lots of friends in Bangalore. There will be many occasions to meet them. If they see you like this, what will they think about us? They will laugh. Hope you remember our status.'

Without getting perturbed, Uttara replied, 'Mummy, I am a student. I am going to study. I will not attend any functions. I do not need this suitcase.'

Rama Rao was very happy with Uttara's steadfastness. He said, 'Uttara, when I was at the Institute, we used to go by train and then take a tonga. Our rooms did not even have fans. But now, I have heard that facilities have improved a lot. It is a privilege to be there. Give your best and make use of every minute you spend there. Your success will be my success. Study well. Don't bring disgrace to the family. I know you are responsible, but . . .' He remembered his good old days and became a bit emotional.

Uttara touched her grandfather's feet and said, 'Don't worry Grandpa, I have always listened to you.'

Venkateshwara Rao decided to drop her to Bangalore as he also had to travel to the city for a meeting the next day. Kamakshi did not have time to accompany her as she had her Rotary Club meeting. So, she signed off simply by saying, 'I wish you all the best.'

Probably in every house, the elders at home will be wishing the same way.

'Uttara, our PA Appa Rao has already opened an account at Canara Bank in the extension counter of the Institute. He has deposited two lakhs. Please use it as you like and tell me before the money gets over,' Kamakshi told her daughter.

'Mummy, I will not require that. I will get a scholarship. For that matter, whosoever studies there will get a scholarship irrespective of their income,' Uttara said, declining her mother's offer.

'If there is money in the bank, it won't hurt you,' Kamakshi said, as she felt sad for her daughter's ignorance.

Uttara descended the marble steps of Lakshmi Nivas. This was the first time she was leaving her dear home. Tears rolled down her cheeks.

Her father walked towards the car, and she followed him in silence. She was unaware of the hurricane the Indian Institute of Science was going to bring into her life. With happiness and a little anxiety, she looked forward to a bright tenure of two years.

Subbu got up early. Between 6 a.m. to 10 a.m. was the only time when they would get corporation water, and it was always his job to fill all the pots and drums at home. Today, as usual practice, he went to the tap.

However, Gowramma said, 'Not today, Subbu; you are going to study at a big college.'

But Subbu did not leave his work.

By the time he got ready to leave for the Institute, Rajanna finished his puja and waited to give prasad to his son.

Gowramma cooked quickly so that her son could eat before leaving. His brother Diwakar ironed his shirt.

Even though they were poor, there was no dearth of love and affection. It was a close-knit family.

Subbu touched his parents' feet.

Gowramma affectionately said, 'May God fulfil all your dreams.'

Subbu walked to the bus stop.

Arvind Shah reached Bangalore's Yeshwanthpur Junction railway station. His back was hurting. He stretched it like a bow. He had travelled from Kanpur to Bangalore in second class. His father, Chandmalji, had insisted on booking a flight ticket but he had said, 'I am a grown-up common man. So, I will travel by train.' It was his motto.

All his family members came to see him off and also because they had not seen a train for a long time.

Arvind's sisters-in-law were relieved. His old aunt was giving her sermon, 'Beta, finish your studies in six months and come back. We do not know what kind of food you get there. You are of a marriageable age. Come and help your father. I am praying to Lord Srinathji for your safe return.'

Another aunt said, 'We are growing old, and we want to see your child.'

One of his nephews said, 'When you are there we will also come, we can go to Mysore Palace.'

His sisters-in-law knew about the Mysore silk saris, but they were aware that this 'impractical' boy would not buy them. So, they did not say anything to him.

Chandmalji was a little worried. He remembered his wife. *If she had been here, she would have handled it much better*, he thought.

Gathering himself, he told his son, 'Arvind, people are people, be it Bangalore, Kanpur or Delhi. Just because you are an idealist, don't think others are also like you. Don't do anything emotionally. I will send some money every month.'

Arvind was not listening to anyone. He was searching for his berth. By that time, he found out that someone else had occupied his seat and was arguing. The train started moving slowly, and he waved at everybody.

It was a reserved compartment for which the tickets were bought months in advance. He had got a lower berth and saw an old lady sitting there. She looked at him with empathetic eyes because she had no reservation. By that time, the ticket collector (TC) arrived, and Arvind started pleading with him, 'Sir, please give this old lady a berth. There might be one at least vacant in this large coach.'

The TC knew the trick of the trade—if the berth was vacant, he would sell it for a higher price. Why would he give it to this old lady?

'No, all berths are full.'

Arvind insisted, 'Can I see the chart?'

'There is no rule which says I should show you,' the TC said and backed out.

Arvind again begged for the berth. This time the TC told him, 'If you are that kind to the old lady, why can't you give your berth to her, and I will allow you to sleep on the floor?'

Arvind accepted immediately, took out his newspaper and started spreading it on the floor. The old lady thanked him enormously. However, by the time he reached Bangalore, he had developed back pain. He took his luggage and called for the rikshaw.

Janaki's travel was easy. Though there were many days before she could join the Institute, she left early. Janaki told her mother, 'Aai, I would rather go early and check the arrangements. I must find out about my tennis and guitar classes also.'

'What are your plans?' asked her father. 'Shall I send some money every month?'

'No, Baba. I will get a scholarship. I have already planned to take up TOEFL and GRE. After I finish my post-graduation, I should be going to the US by September. It is a two-year plan. But I will come to Pune after my first year.'

Dr Paranjape gave her an address card and said, 'This is my friend Prakash Apte's card. He was in the army and has now settled in Bangalore. He used to come to our house when you were a child. You might hardly remember them.'

'No, Baba, I don't.'

'Whenever you have time, you can visit him. They will be very happy.'

However, Meera did not second this idea. Her experience with the Aptes, particularly Prakash's wife,

Sushilabai Apte, was different. Sushilabai had a poor attitude. She came from a very orthodox family and had always looked down upon Meera.

Janaki bid goodbye to her parents and disappeared into the crowd of passengers at the airport.

Those were the days my friend,
I thought would never end.

Uttara hesitantly reached the ladies' hostel. Her father had left after the registration was complete, and she went to the room by herself. The office had already said that in the first year, she would get a shared room and from next year onwards, she could have an individual room. Uttara could not imagine sharing her space as she had always lived in a room of her own, facing the garden. The driver carried her luggage and asked her when he could visit her again. Uttara said, 'I don't think I will require your help any more.'

Her room was on the corner on the first floor. She was about to open the door hesitantly but discovered that it was not locked at all. There was a small chit inserted in the latch. She opened it, 'Dear roommate, welcome. I have gone out and will be back only in the evening. Don't feel shy. The left side bed, table and cupboard are yours. The right ones are mine. Yours, Jani.'

She was surprised and pushed the door. The room was spacious and neatly arranged.

She saw the right side. It had a printed Jaipuri bedsheet, books stacked neatly, photographs of a young couple with a baby and a young lady. There was a book lying on the bed. Uttara opened it and saw Janaki Paranjape's name.

Uttara realized that Jani meant Janaki.

She turned to her bed, opened her luggage and started arranging her clothes and books. She was hoping to meet her roommate, talk to her and perhaps even go to the mess together. She knew that there were many messes, but did not know which one to choose. Uttara remembered her grandpa's talk about the messes, which he frequented during his days at the Institute.

'When I was a student, we had a Bengali mess, Gujarati mess, Madarasi mess etc.,' he had said.

Umesh, his grandson, had made fun of him, saying, 'Grandpa, when you were studying, how many women were there?'

'Oh, there was only one girl on the entire campus. I think her name was Ms Dastoor. She was doing research in paper technology.'

'Yes, you may not remember your thesis, but you remember Ms Dastoor,' Shamala, his youngest granddaughter, poked fun at him.

Venkateshwara Rao also mentioned the messes when he had talked about his student life. 'When I was there, there was A mess for south Indian food, B for north Indian, C for self-service and a separate one for non-vegetarians.'

Again, Umesh had asked, 'How many girls were there, Dad?'

'There might have been ten to twelve. Not many. Not in engineering, mostly researchers, pursuing their PhD. There were a lot of professors from Andhra Pradesh in the Aeronautics Department, several Tamil-speaking professors in the Physics Department and Kannada-speaking professors in the Chemistry Department.'

As Uttara remembered her grandpa's talk, she thought, *now this division has changed. There may be more girls and even a dozen girls in engineering. Even the chairman might have changed.*

When she ventured out, she saw another young woman walk in and vanish into another room. Uttara felt a little strange because the woman did not even acknowledge her presence. She walked down to the main building and saw tall trees competing with their heights in the nice weather. It was evening and the birds were chirping. The surroundings were like a picture painted in green. Uttara felt cold. She returned to her room for a nap.

After a few minutes, a young girl, holding a racket in her hand and humming a Hindi song entered the room. She was wearing a short white skirt and a T-shirt. Uttara thought she looked like Martina Hingis. She introduced herself saying, 'I am Janaki Paranjape, your roommate.'

'Are you Jani?'

'Yes,' she laughed.

Her laugh made Uttara feel quite at home. 'I am Uttara Rao.'

'Come on, Uttara, I will tell you about the messes. I came here three years ago, so people know me. I was supposed to come back at 5, but I wanted to take you for lunch.'

Within a week, Uttara and Janaki understood each other very well. Janaki was a born leader, whereas Uttara was shy. Janaki was an extrovert, and Uttara was an introvert. But they could get along with ease. In Janaki's company, she saw many areas of the Institute.

Janaki would go to the Institute gymkhana every evening to play tennis. She would also practise yoga and focus on her academics.

Uttara felt the whole system was different. There was absolute marking at her university. Students could easily score 60, 70 or 80 per cent. But here, the Institute followed a grading system.

So, even if you scored 85 per cent, it would mean you secured a B grade. In this system, everyone wanted to pull down each other, so that they could get an A grade.

There was one more advantage. A student from any discipline could take any course in the Lecture Hall complex, popularly known as LH. For example, in the numerical analysis class, there would be students pursuing PhDs from the Mechanical and Computer Science departments among others. They had a fantastic library with a large number of books.

Discussions were mainly about scientific discoveries and inventions and not related to money or politics.

The relationship between the teachers and students was very formal, which Uttara found very strange. She remembered in her college, teachers and students interacted frequently and many conversations were informal.

It was time for mathematics class that day, and as per usual, the schedule was sent by email. Uttara sat in her designated place and waited for the professor to come. But no one turned up even after ten minutes. She realized her mistake and turned back. There was only one boy in the gallery hall of the class.

He had put up his feet on another bench and was reading happily. His curly hair and dimples were visible from a distance.

She had seen him many times before in the same class. He saw her, put his book down and said, 'Are you not aware that the class is cancelled?'

'Sorry, I did not check. When is the next class?'

'Until further notice.'

'Then knowing this, why did you come?' asked Uttara.

'I like to sit in the class and read all alone,' he said, smilingly.

'I am Uttara Rao, first year, automation.'

'I am Arvind Shah, first-year, civil.'

A few days later, Uttara noticed a slender girl in a white sari standing near the room next to hers in the hostel building.

She guessed that she might be her neighbour and that her roommate might have stepped out somewhere—just like Janaki had on Uttara's first day. Uttara smiled and said, 'Welcome to the Indian Institute of Science. Come and sit in my room until your roommate comes.'

The girl did not reply.

'I am Uttara Rao, first year, automation.'

'I am Sushma, a chemistry PhD student,' she replied, reluctantly.

'Sushma, Janaki and I go to the same mess. You come with me for tea now. Then you can decide what to do next.'

Sushma did not answer but seemed to be lost in thought.

Though Uttara was not a very talkative person, she tried her level best to make Sushma feel comfortable.

After some time, Sushma's roommate Koushi arrived, and they both went into their room.

That night, Uttara told Janaki the whole thing and asked why Koushi seemed so tense.

'Oh, Koushi's is a large story. She joined six years ago for a PhD and has to finish it this year. Her guide has put tremendous conditions, and she is under a little pressure. She is always in a hurry and doesn't care who is to her left or right. Anyway, Sushma is her roommate, and she doesn't talk much as well. So, they are a good combination.'

Uttara asked, 'Koushi could get a single room due to her seniority, then why was she here and why did she want only that room?'

Janaki replied, 'Because she doesn't want to change the room.'

Months passed. Neither Sushma changed nor Koushi. Uttara and Janaki were immersed in their coursework. They were extremely busy but at the end of the day, they would at least talk for half an hour before going to bed. Talkative Janaki had gathered a lot of news about Sushma. 'It seems Sushma's parents divorced. Her name was the first on the waiting list for PhD admission. One candidate got admission but left for the US. Thus, Sushma got his spot. She had a boyfriend who had promised to marry her, but then, later ditched. All these incidents have made Sushma bitter in life.'

Uttara said, 'Jani, I can't understand how you gather so much information. Sushma has been hurt in every way. I think she should talk and vent it out so that she can feel normal.'

'Everybody is not like me,' replied Janaki, tilted her head towards the right and started reading.

A series of special lectures was published on the notice board.

'Can you give me your pen for a few minutes? I want to write this down,' someone requested Uttara.

Uttara turned back to see; there was a handsome young man.

She gave her pen. He wrote down what he had to and returned the pen saying, 'Thank you, Uttara.'

'How do you know my name?'

'What is special in that? You are the only girl in the class, and you are in our mathematics class as well. Everyone knows you.'

'Oh, I have never noticed you, sorry.'

Oh! Uttara, you are the bright one in the class. You can't see anyone because you only see the board and your book. But we boys can see you and the board, both. And we want to beat you in academics, he said to himself.

Then he smiled and said, 'I am K. Subba Rao, first-year, mechanical.'

The first semester was over, and Uttara had scored excellent marks. Everyone wanted to be her friend. But she was not very keen and would only meet Arvind in the library and Subbu at lectures.

Uttara liked Arvind a lot because of his simplicity and knowledge. Janaki had become almost like her sister. Her grandpa, Rama Rao, was very happy with her progress.

By the time the next semester started, they had all settled, like a fish taking to water.

One day, Sushma stepped into Uttara's room when Janaki was not there. She sat on Uttara's bed and started talking. Although they had come across each other during their first semester, they had never spoken.

Uttara was happy thinking that maybe the ice had broken between them.

'Uttara, how is the new semester?' Sushma asked.

'It is fine,' replied Uttara. 'How are you, Sushma?'

Sushma sighed and said, 'My mood is low. Whatever I have chosen in my life seems to be a waste.'

'Why do you say so?'

'My research work is going nowhere. I'm unable to define my problem. I do not know whether I will be able to complete this. You are lucky. You will finish your course on time and go away.'

Uttara did not know what to reply. Sushma continued, 'I think I am an unfortunate girl. Whatever I touch always turns into failure.'

Sushma continued speaking of negative things. Uttara tried to console her.

'PhD is like this. Everybody undergoes stress in their own way.'

Sushma did not acknowledge Uttara's response and left.

That night, Uttara told Janaki about their conversation and said Sushma was indifferent.

'Uttara, there is no one without difficulties. Everyone will have their own problems, and they have to overcome those.'

Janaki had a different circle. Along with studies, she was always searching for good universities and scholarships in the second semester. She had become good friends with Arvind Shah.

Arvind had a room in N Block—N19.

Subbu would rest in Arvind's room and was his guest in B mess.

That morning, the new course on computers was supposed to start. Uttara was unusually late that day. Janaki had warned her, 'Uttara don't step into the class late. The professor will not like it. It will make a bad impression on the first day.'

That day—a Monday—the queue at the mess was quite long. So, Uttara skipped breakfast and ran to the lecture hall.

Many students were already there, and someone was writing an equation on the board. She believed that he might be a professor.

For courtesy's sake, she asked, 'May I come in, sir? I am late by two minutes.'

He turned back to see her, and said, 'No, you are early by two minutes.'

To her surprise, he was a young teacher.

Everyone laughed and Uttara felt awkward. She hurriedly sat on the first bench.

He started calling out names for attendance. Uttara, who was in deep thought, missed her name and forgot to answer him.

'Hello, are you dreaming?' asked the young man on the dais.

Someone from behind said, 'Yes, she is dreaming about computers. Another student added in a whisper, 'Maybe in a wonderland.'

Uttara felt very uncomfortable.

By that time, a grey-haired man entered the class, and everyone quietened down. The young man soon got down and sat beside Uttara on the same bench.

'Gopal, thanks. You have done half of my work. Let me start from the diagram,' the professor, who had entered the class, said.

Uttara realized that she had mistaken Gopal for the professor. Angry, she was unable to concentrate.

After the class was over, Uttara got up but could not step out as Gopal was sitting next to her.

'Uttara, I am sorry. It was just a joke.'

'I did not like your joke.'

'No one has called me sir till this day. So, I was happy.'

'You cannot make fun of me in front of others, mister,' she said, angry like a serpent.

'I am Gopal Rao, normally people call me Gopi, and I am just about to finish PhD,' he said, in an attempt to introduce himself.

'You may be Gopal or Gopi or whoever. But please give me space,' she said before walking out.

She hardly realized that her long plait had touched Gopal and that he was just about to catch hold of it in mischief.

At lunch, she met Janaki.

'Hi! How was your first class?'

'The class was okay, but I made a mistake. Some Gopal was on the dais, and I thought he was our professor.'

'Oh, he must be Gopal Rao!'

'Jani, do you know him?'

'Of course! I know him very well. We did a French diploma together. He is a very handsome gentleman.'

'I don't know about that, but I felt very awkward in his presence.'

'How can you not say Gopal is a gentleman?' Janaki said, with a question mark on her face.

'What is special about this Gopal Kumar?'

'He is not Gopal Kumar. He is Gopal Rao, one of the finest boys on our campus.'

'Why are you taking his side? Has he bribed you?'

Sometime back, Gopal had requested Janaki to introduce him to her new friend, and though Janaki knew whom he was talking about, she tried to play around a little.

'I have many friends named Gopal. I do not know whom you are talking about,' she had said.

From then on, she had often teased him: 'Hey Gopal, I know whom you are seeing', 'I know you always watch Uttara', 'I know you have changed your mess and started coming here when we come', 'Don't underestimate Janaki's sharpness', so on and so forth.

The semester continued and Uttara was seen more in the class and at the library.

One day, Uttara was sitting with a magazine in the Computer Centre, waiting for the repair on the printers to finish, and Subbu was also there. They were discussing a casual matter. Gopal came in and was quite friendly with Subbu, perhaps because they spoke the same language. Gopal had also ignited a friendship with Arvind. Looking at the three people, Gopal said, 'I want to give you a mathematical problem. Let me see who will solve it quickly.'

Though he spoke to all three, his question was mainly for Uttara.

Arvind was not interested. He was deeply involved in the community house project report.

The moment Uttara heard the word 'problem', she turned her face to Gopal and asked, 'What is that problem?'

'Oh, you cannot solve it in a day!' said Gopal.

'May I know the problem?' said Uttara.

'What is the bet?' asked Subbu.

'The person who loses should invite me for dinner. Suppose one solves the problem, then I will invite that person for dinner.'

'No, I don't want to be a part of any bet, but I want to solve the problem,' said Uttara.

'What is wrong with a bet? It is only an incentive to solve the problem. It is a simple one and not a Kaurava–Pandava-level bet.'

Subbu got the hint in Gopal's challenge and so, he backed out saying, 'Sorry Gopal, I have work, I cannot participate.'

Heads I win, tail you lose. Whether Uttara wins or not, I will have dinner with her.

'I will get back to you,' said innocent Uttara. She never realized what she was getting into.

She took the entire next day to solve the problem successfully. When she was about to go out of the room, Janaki was preparing to go for tennis.

'Janaki, tell your Gopal to come and see me at the Computer Centre as you have his number. I will be there.'

Janaki stopped tightening her shoelace as she could not believe what Uttara had just said.

'Oh, are you meeting him at the Computer Centre?'

'Yes. I have solved the problem,' said Uttara.

'Uttara, please take back the words "your Gopal",' said Janaki and smiled.

'Why?' Uttara was a little curious.

Janaki wanted to say that he was now Uttara's Gopal, and very intelligently, he was preparing a pit to trap Uttara. But as he was a good boy and quite serious about Uttara, she had not tried to stop him.

So, Janaki chose to maintain her silence by not answering Uttara.

Before Janaki could meet Gopal and tell him that Uttara wanted to meet him at the Computer Centre, he was confident that she would certainly come there.

By the time Uttara reached, he was already there. It was a Saturday evening and there was hardly anyone around. The shadows of the tree leaves made playful designs on the walls and the ground. It was a quiet, serene time.

Uttara handed Gopal a paper and said, 'This is the solution to your problem. Now, I want to go back. You lost and I won.'

She just turned back, when he said, 'I agree Uttara that I lost the battle . . . and you have not eaten in the afternoon. At least let us have coffee.'

'How did you know that I have not had lunch!'

. . . *because I know. I waited in the mess, and you did not come. I always follow your activity, Uttara,* said Gopal to himself and smiled.

Uttara had never gone out with any of the boys, except for in the group, like with Subbu, Arvind, Janaki and Gopal.

'I am a gentleman,' said Gopal.

'Of course, I know that. I will come but on one condition.'

Gopal was ready to accept any condition.

'We will split the bill.'

'No, no. That is not correct. Can't I afford a cup of coffee for you?' Gopal resisted.

'You might. But I don't accept treats from unknown people.'

'Am I unknown to you? We meet every day,' said Gopal.

Uttara did not have any answer.

'Okay, I will become a known person to you and introduce myself properly to you. I am Gopal Rao and will finish my PhD early next year. I worked for the Dinshaw Company, which has sponsored my research. I earn a reasonably good salary. I am a Kannadiga and a bachelor,' he said and bowed in courtesy.

Uttara found this very funny, and shyness overcame her. 'I never asked for all these details,' she said.

'Now, may I have your introduction please?' he asked, wanting to know a little about her.

Uttara paused for a minute, thinking: *Do I talk about my father and grandfather? No. I should be identified in my own capacity. No, I will not disclose this.*

'There is nothing special about me. I am Uttara Rao, a student at the School of Automation. I am from Hyderabad. I enjoy computers.' While talking, they walked towards the Coffee House and chose a place to sit. She counted the money from her purse and kept it on the table.

Gopal laughed and took the money.

That night, Janaki quipped, 'It seems you only had coffee with Gopal, and not dinner?'

'How do you know, Jani?' Uttara was very surprised.

'Uttara, please remember that I am three years senior to you on this campus. Your sharp mind did not understand what he said. If you win, he will treat you to dinner and if you lose, you have to treat him to dinner. Either way, two of you would end up having the dinner together.'

Uttara felt shy at her ignorance and lack of common sense.

Uttara, you may now know that Gopal reports to me, Janaki thought.

'Gopal is not what I had thought he is. He is different,' Uttara said.

'Is it? Then how is he?' asked Janaki.

'He is really a gentleman, and he has a good sense of humour.'

'Oh, is it? I did not know that,' laughed Janaki at Uttara's change of opinion.

It was the end of the second semester. There was a long weekend, and Uttara had planned to go home. This semester, Subbu, Uttara and Arvind did not have any combined class. They had chosen their own specialized courses. It was like any other day when Uttara was going to her class, Koushi was busy in the lab and Sushma was staying alone. The room door was slightly ajar. Uttara peeped in and saw Sushma asleep, with her face towards the wall.

When she returned after lunch, Uttara saw that the door was still open as it was in the morning and Sushma was in the same position.

Uttara sensed something wrong and went inside.

Uttara shook Sushma and asked, 'Are you unwell? Shall we go to the doctor?'

Immediately, Uttara let out a scream. Sushma's body was as cold as ice and had become stiff. The froth from her mouth had all dried up.

Janaki heard Uttara screaming and came running.

'Oh my God. Sushma has died,' Uttara shrieked.

Janaki took Uttara away to their room.

Suddenly the hostel turned into a mourning site.

Someone called the police, and another person called the warden.

Everyone was scared. Every room was occupied by five people, instead of two. Soon, the police started inquiring. They wanted to know who her friends were, whom she had last met, what she had said and if they had observed any strange behaviour.

The poor girls told the police of whatever they knew.

But the envelope found below her pillow gave away a crucial piece of information. It read:

I am in depression. I do not have anything to look forward to. I do not want to live. No one is responsible for my death. I am eating cyanide.

Uttara could not recover from the shock. She felt as if a bud was ripped off before it bloomed, birds had stopped chirping, butterflies had stopped flying and life had abruptly ended.

Janaki, who would otherwise be very full of energy and filled with logic, did not speak much to anyone and confined herself to her room.

Though Uttara and Janaki were separated by not more than an arm's distance in their room, they hardly saw each other's face or spoke as usual.

Gopal could understand their emotions and wanted to help them get over their grief.

He took them out for dinner. Uttara tried to recollect her interaction with Sushma and was trying to join the pieces. But Uttara was still unable to accept the reality and cried uncontrollably. Gopal did not stop her, but simply held her hands till she let her sorrow out. She came to a standstill after her eyes were dried of tears entirely. It struck her that her hands were cupped in Gopal's, and it had brought great solace to her mind.

Sumithra observed that Prof. Keshavan was not in a good mood over the last few days. She was reluctant to ask him what the matter was. The normally calm Prof. Keshavan was getting upset over every small thing. One day, he told her to finish a small task, which she quickly did. Yet he was upset with that too.

'You don't even think. You do it immediately,' he had said.

Sumithra did not know how to react. She was the most obedient student. Whatever Prof. Keshavan said was like a rule to her. People used to make fun of her saying that she was married to chemistry, and that an anthill had grown around her like it had around Valmiki, when he was doing his penance for several years.

That day, she was sitting in her lab, eyes full of tears, cleaning the pipette not knowing what to do.

That's when Prof. Keshavan called on her. It scared her more than before. She wondered what harsh words she would have to hear. But Prof. Keshavan looked calm. In a low voice he said, 'Sumithra, I want to tell you a secret. I want to resign from this job. I have been in it for many years. Sorry, today morning, you had made no mistake, but still I yelled at you.'

Initially, she was relieved that she had not made any mistake but later she felt sad hearing that he was planning to quit. Keshavan was not only her PhD guide, but also her mentor.

If he quits, what about her? Who would be her next guide was her worry.

Prof. Keshavan understood her unsaid concern and said, 'Sumithra, don't worry. I am going to IISc Bangalore as a professor.'

'Why, sir?'

'Because my own student Prof. Velayuthan is coming here, as the dean of chemistry. He has married a minister's daughter and has strong political connections. He is not a scholar and does not respect scholarship. I can't work under him.'

'Sir, can't you inform the vice chancellor about this?'

'Our vice chancellor only has posted Velu here. You don't understand all this. The main issue is that I have told IISc that I will come with my student. Will you come with me?'

Sumithra was quiet.

'There is no pressure. I can take any one of my students, but I wanted to give you first preference.'

'Sir, can I have a word at home about this?'

'Of course, you have to. But tell me tomorrow.'

Sumithra always respected people at home and their opinion. But while going home, her mind was in a tizzy. There was a chance she might be going to the Institute which had denied her admission once—luck had knocked at her in the form of Velayuthan. Her father would somehow agree, but she feared her three aunts at home.

After two terms, Sumithra joined IISc.

'Uttara, my friend Prof. Keshavan is joining tomorrow. He is coming with his student Sumithra Iyer. I think she will stay in the room next to yours. Please help her,' Uttara's professor told her.

'Yes, sir, but I have to tell her that Sushma took her own life in this room.'

'That is okay. We are all science students, and we should not bother about such things. Please note that Sumithra has never gone out of Chennai.'

That night Uttara said, 'Jani, don't go for a jog tomorrow. One new girl will check into the next room in the morning.'

'Who is that?'

'Sumithra Iyer from Chennai.'

Both of them suddenly remembered Sushma and saw each other's face.

Next morning when Sumithra entered the hostel, she saw a girl drying her long hair out in the sun, another girl with a bob and green eyes, smiling away. Uttara's diamond studs dazzled in the sun and more than that, her smile.

She approached the new girl and asked, 'Are you Sumithra Iyer?'

'Yes.'

'I am Uttara Rao, and she is Janaki Paranjape.'

Sumithra had never lived in a hostel all alone. Though she had travelled to places like Trichy, Rameshwaram, Srirangam and Tirupathi along with her family, she had never gone anywhere independently. She was exposed to a modern atmosphere, thinking and to an unknown place for the first time. She immediately liked Uttara because she found her pleasant.

As time passed, Uttara fondly thought about her home but never felt homesick. Janaki, it seemed, had forgotten about her home. Arvind was as usual detached from home and hostel. Subbu always felt that the hostel was a better place than his home. The three girls eventually became very good friends.

The first year was soon over. Uttara had fared well. Janaki's performance had been constant. Sumithra got absorbed in chemistry. As the second year dawned, they were all allotted separate rooms. They preferred adjacent rooms in the new hostel. They maintained this friendship that remained the same, even after many years.

Computer science Professor Raghavan wanted to present an international paper in Washington, D.C., for which he was seeking help from students. Normally, MTech students refrained from helping because they had limited time. Some PhD students do take up such avenues but if they are in their final year of submission, then they too avoid. Prof. Raghavan had taught Gopal; he knew he would oblige and offer help.

He asked Gopal, 'If you have submitted your thesis, can you please help me out?'

'Sir, please don't worry about it. I will definitely do your work. But I may need an assistant to finish it fast.'

'Whom do you want?'

'Sir, your student Uttara Rao. She does a good job and is dedicated.'

'Oh. That is not a problem at all. If I tell her, she will agree. By the way, Gopal, I am aware that you are submitting your papers in civil engineering, but you are so good at computers. Why don't you do another PhD in computer science?'

'No, sir, I like civil engineering. To be more precise, in my civil designs, I require computers. Without that it is difficult to do structural design. My company has sent me here, and I intend to finish PhD in three years.'

'Are you going back to your company?'

'Yes, sir, there is a bond which I can forfeit with money. But I will not do that. I will always remember the people who helped me.'

'The decision is yours. I will talk to Uttara, and you can start the work today itself.'

Sumithra was deep into reference work in the lab and had lost track of time. She realized it was closing time and felt rather scared as it had become quite dark. The Institute was a safe and a well-lit place, but she had never walked alone at that time. She grabbed her books and started hurrying towards the hostel. She felt someone was following her. It added to her fear. She increased her pace of walking, but she felt the other person also hastened behind her. She did not have the courage to look back. She remembered the worst scenes from old movies and started praying to God with the hope that she reached her room safely. She also vowed to offer *vade male*—a garland made of urad dal—to Lord Hanuman.

Someone called, 'Hey, stop. Don't run. I saw a snake here an hour before. I just wanted to warn you and help if need be.'

Sumithra turned back. In the frail light, she saw a thin, tall man. He was wearing a khadi kurta and jeans. He introduced himself, 'Don't be scared. I am Arvind Shah, second year, civil.'

Then he looked at her face. Pearls of sweat were all over Sumithra's face and her complexion was competing with the red of her sari.

For the first time Arvind had looked at a girl's face so clearly. He felt she was very beautiful.

With a trembling voice, she said, 'I am Sumithra Iyer from physical chemistry lab.'

The new batch of first-year students arrived on the campus. By this time, the final year postgraduate students had formed their own groups.

Sumithra did not go anywhere except for the south Indian canteen. As Gopal and Uttara were working together during the evening hours, they would eat together at the same mess, either at A, B or C.

One day, Sumithra asked Uttara, 'I need some help with computers. One week is enough. I don't want to do a semester. Can you please help me?'

'I would have, but I don't have time. Arvind is a good fellow. He will readily help anyone. I can talk to him.'

'Is it the same Arvind of civil engineering?'

'How do you know him?' Uttara asked, a little surprised.

Sumithra explained the whole incident, following which Uttara said, 'Yes, he can go to any extent to help people.'

Uttara spoke to Arvind about it, and he agreed.

Every day they would sit in a corner of the library and Arvind would teach Sumithra.

It was a new experience for them because neither of them had interacted with the opposite gender in solitude, unlike Janaki and Uttara.

Apart from learning computer science, they developed a good friendship with each other.

It was Sunday morning. Uttara and Sumithra were not yet up. The previous night, they had worked until late in their respective labs.

Janaki woke up at six, completed her jog and dressed up in a salwar kameez. She peeped into Sumithra's room and saw that she was still lying in her bed but reading a book.

'Hey Sumi, you do not have anything else to read other than chemistry?'

'Oh, that is my life. What is your life, Jani?'

'For me, the sky is the limit. I have so many things to do. You have to enjoy every bit of those. Life is a colourless painting. You can paint it the way you want. People with enthusiasm paint it colourfully. Pessimistic people do it differently. I always look at it cheerfully.'

Listening to Janaki, Sumithra woke up from her bed and said, 'You have not seen real life. There is helplessness, failure, bindings, suffering and obligations. You have always won everything, so you don't understand.'

'Not that Sumi, I believe that life is a game, whether you win or lose it, you have to play. Life is a battle. Whether you get success or failure, it is all your effort. When you lose, you can't sit there. You have to get over it and start playing the next one. This is my perception.'

Looking at Janaki's energy and that she was dressed up, Sumithra jokingly asked, 'Are you going to play or fight a war?'

'Neither of them. I am going to my father's friend's house,' she replied.

'Oh. Who all are there?'

'I really do not know. It is an obligation, and so, I must go.'

'All the best, Jani. Have a nice time,' Sumithra wished her, with mischief in her voice.

'Sumi, no thanks,' Janaki yelled as she walked out of the room.

Prakash Apte had built a small house with a big garden in R.T. Nagar. Janaki had not bothered to visit the Aptes for a year. Dr Paranjape always reminded her and today, she thought she could finish that task of visiting them. It was easy to trace their house. When she entered, she saw a nice tulsi pot, decorated and worshipped, indicating the religious nature of the owner, and there was also a tennis court.

She rang the bell, but there was no response. She had called and told the Aptes that she would visit them, but now, there was no one opening the door.

She felt awful. It was Sunday—masala dosa day at the hostel mess. However, Janaki did not miss it; she was bored of eating it for five years now; but she did miss her long Sunday jog, almost repenting giving it up to wait at someone's door.

She rang the bell for the last time, before going back.

She had almost turned away when she heard some noise, someone climbing down the stairs.

When the door opened, she was surprised at the sight of a young man in his shorts and without a shirt. He had messy hair and a vessel in his hand.

He felt ashamed and said, 'Wait a minute. I will be back.'

In the meantime, Janaki looked at the court. She felt as if someone tended to it every day. The garden was beautiful. At that time, the boy went up, brushed his teeth, changed his clothes and came down again.

He said, 'I am Nakul Apte, Mr Prakash Apte's son. My parents have asked me to tell you that they will be late today, but I forgot.'

'Can I get a glass of water?' Janki asked. She was tired of waiting for such a long time.

'Please come inside.'

He did not realize that he should have called her inside earlier.

The house was very neat and tidy. Nakul brought a glass of water.

'My parents had to suddenly go to a condolence meeting. They may come soon.'

'Thank you. But I will leave now. When they come, you please tell them that Dr Paranjape's daughter visited them.'

'May I know your name please?' he asked.

'I am Janaki Paranjape. I study at IISc.'

Nakul tried to stop her until his parents came. 'Please stay back, my parents will come any time now. Or they may feel bad.'

Janaki did not know how to continue the conversation.

'Who plays tennis in your house?' she asked.

'I play. Do you play?'

At last, there was a little energy in the conversation now.

'Yes, I do,' Janaki replied, coyly.

'Then shall we play a game?' Nakul asked, glad that he had a good reason to keep her occupied.

'But I am not wearing the dress for it,' she said. Janaki was not used to playing, wearing a salwar kameez.

'Oh, it is not Wimbledon.'

For Janaki, the urge to play the game was more than the discomfort she felt about her outfit.

For Nakul, it was otherwise. He only wanted to engage her till his parents returned.

As soon as they started playing, he realized that she was a serious player and played much better than him.

After the game, he offered her a cold coffee and talked about himself.

'Where do you work?' she asked.

'As you know, my father was in the military. I have gone around many places. Schooling at Gwalior, engineering from Delhi, MBA from IIM Ahmedabad. Right now, I am working in the marketing team of a software company.'

Though he insisted that Janaki have breakfast, she did not accept. She always stayed away from becoming friends with unknown people.

The Aptes returned home from the condolence meet by then. Prakash Apte insisted that Janaki stay back, but she said she had an important assignment and got ready to leave.

'Please come again. We can play another game,' said Nakul

'Sure,' said Janaki and left.

Uttara, Arvind and Subbu took the same class in linear programming. There was a test the next day. Their library had only one copy of an important course book on that subject, and Arvind had reserved it.

However, when he went to take the book in the evening, he did not find it. He did not know what to do. The librarian checked and confirmed that it had not been issued to someone and perhaps was not in the right place. Arvind walked out disappointed.

Uttara was standing outside and asked him, 'Arvind, what happened?'

'I had reserved a Lee book, but it is not there. I was so dependent on that book for tomorrow.'

'Don't worry. I have that book. I had purchased it from outside. You can take it.'

'But you also have the same test tomorrow.'

'That is fine. I am already prepared. Come with me to the hostel.' They went together to her hostel. Arvind sat in the reception area. He thought it was so easy for Uttara to help anyone. Invariably, he thought of his sisters-in-law who were extremely competitive and never generous towards each other. They were so self-centred that they could not even think of helping someone. Maybe education expands your horizon in life and makes you large-hearted. By the time he had finished mulling, Uttara got him the book.

The next day, after the test was over, Arvind was extremely happy and satisfied. He asked Subbu, 'How did your test go?'

'Okay,' he replied, not sharing how he had actually written the test.

'Mine was fine too,' said Uttara. She never exaggerated her marks or strengths. Hers was the case of under-promising and over-delivering.

Subbu left for the library. Arvind and Uttara were discussing some matters when Arvind suddenly remembered that he had to return books to the library. While at the counter, he saw Subbu placing the Lee book back in its place. In a fraction of a second, he understood what had happened. He could not believe that Subbu would do this, knowing very well that Arvind had reserved the book.

This is what happens in relative grading and when one fosters unhealthy competition.

Arvind thought again, *who says higher education makes you magnanimous?* That is not true. Subbu was very friendly with him, but when it came to his own personal progress, he could jump any ethical line.

Helplessly, Subbu smiled.

'Why did you do that, Subbu?' asked Uttara when they both met for coffee. 'We are all good friends. Arvind was so upset yesterday. He told me about it.'

'Uttara, you do not know what poverty means. That is the reason you talk like this. You and Arvind can afford to buy a Lee book. But I cannot. Poverty is helplessness. I am saving every rupee to complete my course. I am just waiting to have a comfortable life. Nobody appreciates your hard work. People see only money.'

With a neutral mind, Uttara said, 'You do not know how rich people live. They are in their own bubble, away from reality. Their personal lives are quite complex. To maintain their status, they must struggle. You are an intelligent person and a hard worker. You will definitely get out of poverty. But you should remember that once you are out of it, you should not forget to be a good human.'

While coming to the hostel, she remembered her family. At the big dining table, the conversations were so different. Her elder brother, Umesh, who was going to be the heir, behaved like a boss. His ideas were centred around which car or bike to buy or when he could throw a party to impress people.

Her mother, Kamakshi, often tried to hide old age behind make-up and compete with other ladies in her circle. Her sister, Shamala, had once said, 'I want to marry a rich and handsome businessman, who is established and does not have parents. He should just give me good money to spend and not account for it. I want a four-day wedding, and it should be the best wedding in Hyderabad. I want my dresses from Anita Dongre and Rohit Bal collections and none of them should be repeated.'

Uttara had laughed at this and said, 'So impractical. I think you should marry an old, orphaned man, who doesn't bother about how you spend and doesn't care. To get that kind of money is not easy. Look at our own company. Unless we are profitable, we cannot spend like this. I feel it is important to marry a person who cares for your feelings and respects you. That brings respect to the family. I totally disagree. I will not change an iota of my opinions.'

Her brother always dreamed of marrying a rich girl. He had said, 'If I marry another contractor's daughter, then I can take care of both businesses and will have plenty of money. I can also get an equal amount of loan from the bank.'

Uttara had discouraged him.

'Umesh, stay grounded. The way you are talking will happen only if God is willing. Why will a girl accept you if she is not compatible with you? Why will her father allow you to take care of their business?'

If not guided at the right time, children become lazy and self-centred. Wealth never stays in such a family for long. It dries up soon.

Uttara's hostel-mate Parvathy was getting married in Hyderabad, and she had invited all her friends.

Subbu was hesitant because he did not have much money for the travel expenses. 'Where shall we stay?' he asked.

'In Uttara's house,' said Janaki.

'Come let us go and stay in the *kalyana mantapam*. There will be enough place and food,' said Sumithra.

'Let us go by train. It will be fun,' said Arvind.

'Let us go by budget airlines. It will be fast and cheap,' said Janaki.

All of them agreed.

Sumithra was a little perturbed. She said, 'I did not bring many saris here.'

'Don't worry. Bring a red, black and white blouse. I will give you my sarees,' said Uttara.

They all travelled to Hyderabad. It was the first flight for Arvind, who had never taken one owing to his principles; for Subbu, who had never been on one due to financial restraints; and for Sumithra, who had never boarded one due to social constraints.

Janaki and Uttara were used to it.

There was a Toyota car waiting for them at Hyderabad airport. When they reached Lakshmi Nivas, apart from Arvind, all the others were surprised. Looking at it, Janaki wondered how Uttara had shared the room with her. The food served at her home was so different from the mess, and Janaki wondered how Uttara was having it. Subbu did not have words to describe how he felt.

Wearing a simple cotton saree, living like a middle-class girl, and not talking about her personal life, no one had imagined that she would be rich. Janaki was aware that Uttara belonged to a business family but did not expect her to be so elite.

Subbu said, 'I am sorry. I did not know your background.'

'Why sorry, I am just like you all,' said Uttara.

And they were planning to take a train!

'While returning, you please come by business class,' said Subbu.

'No, I never do such things. I am one among us,' defended Uttara.

'It is okay, Subbu. Let us live like ordinary people and learn things in life,' Arvind added.

Yes, life indeed taught Uttara many lessons later.

Dharwad in North Karnataka is famous for its peda, buffalo milk, and most importantly, Hindustani Classical Kirana Gharana.

Gopal had grown up in Dharwad and naturally, he had fallen in love with the music of Kirana Gharana. It has produced great musicians like Abdul Karim Khan, Hirabai Barodekar, Gangubai Hangal, Bhimsen Joshi and many more.

In memory of Sawai Gandharva, who popularized the Kirana Gharana, every year a musical festival was conducted at Kundgol, a few kilometres away from Dharwad.

Hindustani singers from all over India connected with the Kirana Gharana come to Kundgol and sing with great pride and devotion. The villagers who work in the fields, who look simple and ignorant, are actually connoisseurs of music. This festival goes on from night to morning. This is conducted in the house of Kundgolkar, a huge *wada* that is at least five hundred years old. Nobody invites anyone. Occasionally, there might be tea and water. But there is no other hospitality. It is simply like music flowing like a river, from dusk to dawn. The whole atmosphere is serene and informal.

Gopal's parents lived in Dharwad. His father, Prof. Mahadev, taught literature at Karnatak College and his mother Sukanya was a part-time schoolteacher. They were staunch supporters of the music festival, and Gopal grew up with the same passion. They had three children, that is what they say. But the truth is they have only two sons.

About twenty years ago, Prof. Mahadev was transferred to a government college near Dandeli. There, an unusual incident occurred. The woman, who would clean their house and help them with daily chores, died during childbirth. Since her husband had already left her, the child was orphaned. Mahadev and Sukanya adopted that child. They promised the woman that they would look after the baby as their own, and so they did. Thus, Meenu grew up with the two boys and never knew about her biological parents, until one day, someone told her. She was a little disturbed and started feeling insecure. Sukanya and Mahadev sat with her and explained what had transpired. They said, 'You were born to someone else, but you are with us as our daughter. You are like Krishna, and we are Yashodha and Nanda.' Meenu understood what Mahadev and Sukanya had said. She grew up to be a good classical singer, and everybody encouraged her. Then, one day, when Gopal was at IISc, she said that she wanted her brothers to attend her debut at the Sawai Gandharv festival.

Gopal announced, 'My sister Meenu is going to make her debut in classical music. On behalf of my family, I would like to invite all of you to Dharwad. It is on the weekend. We can take the night train and reach Dharwad by morning. We can take the Sunday night train and on Monday morning we will return to the Institute. The train passes through Yeshwantapur. It won't be difficult.'

Arvind, who was fond of classical singing, raised his hand first. Janaki who was from Pune, the seat of Hindustani Classical music, was the next. Subbu, though he did not enjoy much Hindustani, agreed to come for company. Sumithra had never heard of Hindustani, so she was curious. Gopal looked at Uttara. She said she hadn't seen the place and agreed to join.

This was a great change for Uttara. Firstly, she was travelling in sleeper class for the first time. Secondly, she wanted to know more about Gopal's family. Thirdly, she wanted to know how common people live and behave during the festival. She was used to VIP seats and huge air-conditioned auditoriums and was looking forward to her first-ever open-air music festival.

Gopal's parents had a fairly good house and a beautiful garden. Sukanya indulged quite a bit in gardening. They were very happy to welcome their guests without any fuss. They arranged a bedroom for the girls and Gopal and his brother shared their bedroom with the boys.

Meenu was the apple of Mahadev's and Sukanya's eyes, but one could make out that her features were different from all others in the family. Sukanya gifted the guests Dharwad sarees and peda packets before all of them proceeded to the music festival. Meenu sang well, and they also got a chance to hear the singing of Pandit Bhimsen Joshi and many more stalwarts.

The whole atmosphere was effortless. Janaki was used to it, but definitely not Sumithra or Uttara. Arvind was indifferent to everything else and was enjoying the music.

Uttara was thinking about how her family maintained a distance from their domestic helpers, without enquiring about their personal lives and well-being. She felt bad. *I also have become part of the system unknowingly*, she thought. *I have always been busy with my studies and have never bothered about anything else.*

She realized why Gopal was so different, how extraordinary his parents were and how well-knit their family was.

Sukanya, who had come among Gopal's friends, struck up a conversation. She said, 'I always adjusted my career depending on my children's. When my children were young, I worked part-time. When they were in high school, I worked full-time. Now, I work overtime. I must have lost good money in such deals, but to spend time with my children at a tender age, sharing my knowledge with them and giving them good values was my aim. Now, Meenu goes for *riyaz,* and I accompany her each time. So again, I have opted to work part-time. All my three children have never disappointed me.'

Uttara remembered her mother, fiercely competing for the sake of status and never spending any time with the children. She and her siblings had spent more time with their drivers, domestic help, cooks and caretakers at home.

She was in awe of Gopal's family bond and lifestyle.

Youth is the greatest period in one's life.

Many things happen unknowingly.

People fall in love quickly and regret it for the rest of their lives.

The attraction between the two genders reaches its zenith in that period and slowly fades away.

For the sake of love, many things have happened and created history.

Many wars have been fought, poems written, sculptures have been made, much music composed and dances choreographed.

Everything is colourful when in love. It is Holi, a riot of colours, every day.

There is no logic when someone falls in love. Gopal fell in love with Uttara. He was attracted to her goodness, intelligence, simplicity, and maybe even for some unknown reason.

Uttara was not expressive, but she fell in love with Gopal too. She knew he came from a humble background, but still the attraction was magnetic. Probably, he was the first person in her life who expressed his love through his eyes.

It is often said that if more people are involved in a task, the work time is reduced by half.

If Uttara and Gopal had been assigned a task individually, they may have perhaps finished it in fifteen days. But together, they took four weeks. Smart Janaki knew by this time that Uttara and Gopal were paired. But she never interfered. After all, they were adults. Whether they would get married or not was best left to them. Subbu was also aware of this. He was envious of Gopal because he believed he had made a 'priced catch'. Subbu considered Uttara a catch, whereas Gopal considered her a good human being.

Arvind was unbothered by the pairing. Sumithra did know about this and was a little worried because she was aware of the difficulties of such a marriage. She silently prayed to the Lord.

Bangalore Chamber of Commerce had organized a lecture series with Mr Venkateshwara Rao, Uttara's father, as the speaker. Uttara came to the IISc bus stop and had strictly instructed her father to not send the driver. Of late she was impressed by Arvind's simple way of life. To her surprise, Gopal was also there.

'How come you are all alone? Where are your maidens?' teased Gopal.

'I am not a princess,' laughed Uttara.

'Where are you going?' Gopal said. He wanted to use this chance to spend time with her.

'I am going out for some work,' Uttara said, without sharing many details.

Gopal made a wild guess, 'Majestic Circle?'

'Yes.'

'Going for a movie?' he tried to guess next.

'Would I go alone if it were a film? No, I have some other work.'

'Do you want company? I will come,' Gopal said and pushed aside his work.

'Mr Gopal Rao, I don't watch movies with bachelors.'

'Ms Uttara Rao, it is true, I am a bachelor, but I am also your friend.'

Both laughed.

The bus arrived and both got on it.

Gopal purchased the tickets—'two to Majestic'—and continued his conversation.

'I would like to watch a movie with a young unmarried girl.'

'You might like that, but I would not.'

Normally, Uttara would not talk so much, but by now, she was comfortable enough with Gopal to speak without any hesitation.

They got down at the right place and both walked towards the Chamber of Commerce.

'Uttara, are you attending this lecture?'

Gopal was almost sure why she had come.

'Yes,' Uttara confirmed.

'I am a civil engineer, and it is my subject, that is why I have come. But why did you come?' Gopal was curious.

'I came just like that. What are your plans after the lecture? said Uttara.

'Oh, good you reminded me. I have to treat you to dinner for losing the bet,' said Gopal.

Uttara remembered the cleverness behind the bet and laughed.

'Oh, I do remember.'

'Then, shall we go to Kamat?'

'No.'

'Kaveri?'

'No.'

'Then tell me your choice.'

'Not today.'

Gopal felt Uttara was slipping away, like a fish into the water.

'You may say Hotel Ashoka, but I don't want to go there.'

'In that case, we will split the bill.'

Now, Gopal was angry.

'Uttara, if you do not want to have dinner with me, it is fine. But don't give reasons.'

'Gopal, please be quiet. The speaker can come any time.'

'Oh, I don't care. This speaker is well-connected with politics. He uses that to get contracts and is always worried about his status. They always want yes-boss kind of people.'

'How do you know this?'

'We are their competitors. Dinshaw Construction Company where I work is any day superior to them. But we lose contracts because we are ethical.'

'Then why did you come here?' asked Uttara.

'To know how they don't walk the talk. So, I can tell my colleagues how foolish they are,' he said, adding, 'By the way, why have you come? This is not your subject.'

Uttara paused a minute, took a deep breath, and said, 'Because the speaker is my father.'

Suddenly, Gopal felt as if he was struck by lightning. He stood like a stone statue.

Before he could form a reply, a person called Uttara and took her to the first row.

'Okay Gopal, see you tomorrow at dinner,' she said and vanished without waiting for his reply.

Gopal sat through the lecture, but his ears and mind were closed. His head was ringing from the shock he had just received, his chest was heavy, and his face had reddened with anxiety.

If he had known that Uttara was the daughter of Venkateswara Rao, he would have maintained a distance despite liking her.

From her simplicity, he presumed that she was from an ordinary middle-class family like his own; so, he allowed himself to fall in love.

At home, his mother was always pressuring him to get married.

She had said, 'Gopal, you do not have any family responsibility. You are finishing your PhD, and it is time for you to settle down. If you have chosen anyone, tell me. I will go and talk to them. Otherwise, I will search for a suitable match for you.'

He had not uttered a word about Uttara to anyone openly.

Now, he was really worried.

He had used his choicest words to describe Venkateswara Rao and his company.

He anticipated that Uttara would neither see him nor meet him from now on. Even if she met, she would certainly give him a good thrashing and would walk away.

'What an impractical fool I am,' he cursed himself.

He decided to seek Uttara's apology and not meet her anymore. He decided to allow time to heal his wound. He also thought it was better to tell his mother to find a girl for him.

On the evening of the next day, Uttara went to the Computer Centre, but Gopal did not talk to her. Uttara herself started talking as though nothing had happened.

'Yesterday, I had to go with my father for dinner. That is why I had to turn your offer down. Are you upset?'

'No.'

'As per our bet, shall we go one of these days?'

'No.'

'Kamat?'

'No.'

'Okay, I will not split the bill. Let us go wherever you want,' Uttara said in an attempt to pacify Gopal, but he did not respond.

'Let us not meet here onwards,' Gopal said.

'Why?' Uttara asked, worried.

'You know the reason.'

'We must not talk here. Let us go near the statue.'

'No. There is nothing to discuss.'

'Gopal, let us talk it out. Many problems can be solved by talking,' she insisted.

They came to the main building and sat on the steps below the statue.

With sadness, Gopal said, 'Uttara, please excuse me. If I knew that you were the daughter of such a rich man, I would have refrained from developing any feelings for you.'

'Have I, at any point, behaved like a rich man's daughter?'

'No. And that is precisely the reason I got carried away.'

'But Gopal, I did not make any wrong decision. I was not carried away. I met your family, and I am aware of all the circumstances. And I have knowingly allowed my feelings to continue for you.'

'Uttara, think over it. Emotions do not stay for a long time. You will regret it later. I may never become a big person in real life. You should be optimistic, but you should also know the reality.'

'Gopal, I am ready to face it.'

'Your parents will never agree.'

'Yes, they will never agree. They will make my life miserable and will not give me even a piece of their property as inheritance.'

'Uttara, I don't want any money from you. God has been kind to me, and I have always had a content life. But you do not know what a middle-class life is. Take time. No hurry.'

'Ever since I have come from Dharwad, I have been thinking about it. And I knew this day would come soon. I had also anticipated your reaction. Gopal, as long as you love and respect me, give me space and stand by me, my decision will remain the same.'

Gopal was moved upon listening to Uttara's words. It brought to surface his sense of humour . . . he said, 'This Abhimanyu will do whatever Uttara wants.'

Uttara took her right hand, put it on Gopal's mouth and said, 'Let my Abhimanyu live a long, fulfilling life.'

The tall trees, the Tata statue, the main building, the green meadow, all nodded in approval.

Nakul Apte would often call Janaki to play tennis, and she would occasionally go. They got used to each other's style of playing. However, there was no romance on the cards for Janaki.

Janaki secured a PhD spot at UCLA, United States, with a scholarship. Subbu got a job in one of the Diwanji companies. Uttara did not want to apply anywhere because her future depended on Gopal's. Arvind applied for a job in a Delhi company that was working on a rural housing project in Madhya Pradesh. Sumithra was yet to complete her PhD.

It was the end of July and time for all of them to depart. For the last time, they all met under the neem tree, near Canara Bank.

Uttara said, 'I don't know how quickly the years have passed. I still feel as if I came to the Institute only a few months ago. It would be nice to meet every year, but you never know where we will be. Let's make a pact. Whether or not we meet in between, shall we all . . . all meet after twenty-five years, if possible, in the same place?'

Janaki added, 'Just meeting and saying hello is very simple. In the next twenty-five years we do not know what we will be. Perhaps, we will all be parents, grey-haired and maybe, successful.'

'Yes, that is the reason we have to reflect on the journey of life and discuss,' said Subbu.

'Is this our last meeting?' asked Sumithra.

'Not really, we will have one more meeting, during Uttara and Gopal's wedding. But nobody knows when and where?' said Janaki.

'Oh, is it! I never knew this,' Arvind said.

Oh! Arvind, you are such a great soul. You will not understand all this, thought Sumithra.

'Congrats,' said Subbu to Uttara. He smiled within, feeling proud that he had predicted this long back.

Janaki said, 'Uttara, you must marry within two months before I go to the US. I cannot come to the wedding after that.'

'Though I have come later than all of you, I will have stay here for more years,' said Sumithra.

'Let us all eat together in the mess today,' said Gopal.

'Uttara is the one who will manage our next meeting, after twenty-five years. It is not hard, we have emails. Who knows, in twenty-five years we may get some other tool which might be faster than a call or email,' said Gopal.

'Let Gopal be a witness for today's meeting and the one after twenty-five years,' said Janaki.

'In that case, let us debit all our lunch expenses from Gopal's account,' said Janaki cheerfully. The others joined her.

It is hard for any human to accept harsh reality.

Extremely ambitious people are usually selfish.

Selfish people don't care for others' feelings.

Neither is life extremely hard, nor is it completely easy.

It is a combination of both.

Uttara left the hostel with some anxiety. Though she had done well in her exams, she knew that her toughest exam would be at home. She was unlike Janaki or Arvind, who could easily do what they wanted. By nature, she was calm, and fights would scare her.

Once at her home, at the dinner table, she was waiting to broach the topic, but Kamakshi outsmarted her.

'Uttara, now you have finished your degree. We have waited for a long time. Your grandfather has always insisted that we should not talk about your marriage until you complete your studies. All my friends' daughters are already married.'

'Do you have anyone on your mind?' Venkateshwara Rao asked Kamakshi.

'Yes, we have shortlisted two–three grooms from here and a few NRIs. All these boys are highly qualified and more or equal to us in status,' said Kamakshi.

'Mom, what is their status like?'

'Good assets, good name in society and respect in the business world.'

'How do you know they will be compatible with me?'

'We will arrange meetings. You will have a choice. And after all, marriage is an adjustment,' her father said.

'No Daddy, I cannot judge anybody in half an hour. They can put on a show at that time. And I want to know my partner better. What are his likes, dislikes, what he wants out of this marriage and such.'

'Uttara, any marriage in our society is like a business venture.'

'No, I disagree. It has to be from the heart, and I have followed my heart and have found a groom for myself.'

Her mom was aghast. 'What? At last, you have ditched us! Which community is he from? What religion? What does the boy do? Where is his family?'

'Whose son? What business are they into?' asked her father.

'What assets do they own?' Kamakshi asked sharply.

'I thought you went to study. I did not know that you went there to search for a groom for yourself,' added Umesh.

Uttara slowly started, 'His name is Gopal, a PhD from IISc. His father is a professor.'

'Where is he working?'

'Dinshaw Constructions,' she said, hesitantly.

'Are you mad? Of all the people, how did you accept him? You know that they are our stiff competitors. Whenever there is a tender, they apply and snatch our project. You have seen that many times, isn't it? And now, you want to marry him?' said her father, furiously.

'Uttara, you have not seen life. You have just stepped out of your home. You are impractical. Think before you commit,' her grandpa said in a cajoling voice. 'You take a year off and go to America. Enroll in a course there. And after that, still, if you feel like marrying him, you can go ahead.'

Out of sight will be out of mind, was his vision.

'I am an adult. I thought about it for a long time and only then I have made this decision,' Uttara said with affirmation.

'If you have already decided without asking anyone at home, then I don't want to talk to you. What a shame you have brought upon me. My friends will laugh at me,' Kamakshi stood up and left the room.

'Oh, you are only informing us, that's all,' taunted Umesh.

'Uttara, you do not understand. You are a big catch for him. You are well educated, from a great family and have good status along with money. Any boy would like to marry you,' said her father.

'That is not true, Daddy. Gopal did not know that I was your daughter. No one in the Institute knew about my financial status. I kept it that way because I was aware that people would want to marry me for money.'

Though Uttara knew the result, the process was making her sad.

Her grandpa interfered, 'If she is so keen, in that case, let her marry him after one year. Before that, we will also meet the boy and his family and assess them.'

'Grandpa, you don't understand,' Umesh said. 'If he wants to marry Uttara, then he should leave Dinshaw Company and join our business instead.'

Uttara knew that he would never do it. She knew how Gopal looked down upon Venkateshwara Rao's company and even if he joined them for her sake, he would leave within a month.

'Will he sign a prenuptial agreement?' asked Umesh.

'What is that?' asked grandpa.

'It is a legal agreement before marriage. In the case of divorce, neither of the parties can claim anything from the other. Then we don't have to give any asset to him.'

'That means you are thinking of divorce, even before getting married?' grandpa asked.

'It is a common practice these days. It secures the families of the bride and the groom,' said Shamala.

Uttara said, 'Gopal will sign it happily, but I want to sign a document before that. I don't want any money from this house. You have given me a good education, looked after me for twenty-five years and have always given me the freedom to do what I want. Is this not more than enough? I know Gopal. He can always earn money. Maybe not as much as this family, but we will be reasonably well off and content in life.'

She left the table and went inside.

The discussions went on for many weeks. But Uttara won in the end. Much against everybody's wishes, they decided to perform the wedding in Tirupati.

Mahadev and Sukanya felt stressed around the bride's family and did not expect anything from them. Neither did Venkateshwara Rao show any respect to the groom or his family. It was like finishing an unwanted task. The joy was more on the groom's side because everyone liked Uttara. Gopal and Uttara were lost in their own world. As the wedding took place before September, all their friends, including Janaki, attended it. It was a simple and short ceremony.

Kamakshi gave some diamond ornaments to show off. However, Gopal instructed Uttara to return all the ornaments received from her parents' side. Uttara happily agreed and gently touching the studs she had worn, said, 'I don't mind giving away the ornaments, except the ones given by my grandmother.'

Thus, Uttara left for Dharwad.

Kamakshi felt like she was sending her daughter to exile.

Arvind received a cold welcome when he returned to Beespur. While going he had carried one suitcase, but while returning, he had only half of it. He had donated his clothes to the poor people on the platform and had only books with him. One of his sisters-in-law said, 'We look after him so much; he has got a scholarship and still he did not buy even a sari for each of us. So ungrateful.'

Chandmalji felt it was time to speak to Arvind as an adult.

'Arvind, you are of marriageable age now. We will start a book publishing business for you. Run your own business. You need not stay here. I will buy a new house for you. You marry a girl of your choice and lead an independent life. I want to separate my assets for everybody while I am alive. Later, nobody will help you.'

'Baba, starting a publishing house has nothing to do with the love for knowledge. It is only a business. I do not want any independent company. I will go to Delhi and work.'

'What job? Which company?'

'Mehta Company in Delhi. It is not a big company. They will give a very small salary.'

'If you set up a company, you can pay a hundred such people,' his father tried to reason.

'Baba, I don't want to have my own company. I am not joining this company for the sake of money. My expenses are limited. I am joining this company because they are building houses for the tribal people. I have done MTech in this subject and can apply my knowledge practically.'

'Beta, life is not as simple as you think. A company may not follow what it advertises. Every company's ultimate motto will be profit-making. Wherever there is profit, the company works there. I have said as much as I could have. However, the decision is yours. Ultimately one day, you will realize that what I am saying is the truth. But unfortunately, I might not be there to see that. I have a lot of experience with real life, that is the reason I can tell you.'

Chandmalji got upset and left.

Arvind left for Delhi the same night.

It was the first time in Mumbai for Subbu. His parents had come to the airport to see him off. He had gone with a suitcase, a good postgraduate degree and tremendous confidence. With these things in tow, he wanted to try his luck in this magic city of Mumbai.

However, upon reaching, he felt Mumbai was cramped, unlike Bangalore.

Arvind reached Delhi. He had many relatives in the city, but he did not go there. Instead, he rented a *barsati* in Greater Kailash II and joined the job the very next day.

He observed that several people simply sat there and talked about rubbish things. There were hardly any useful conversations. The boss would come and leave whenever he wanted.

The south Indian receptionist Meenakshi spoke to him very well, read his biodata and thought he might be a good 'catch'. So, she called him for a coffee. Arvind said,

'Please don't call me. Just continue with your work.' To which, Meenakshi commented, 'He's new to the office so he behaves as if this is his home. A new washerman not only washes the clothes but also the donkey. Over the years, he doesn't even wash the clothes.'

When Arvind heard this, he ignored it.

Life was entirely different in the office. His links with the outside world were Sumithra's emails and his father's calls. Arvind felt life had become boring. He would have been happy if he could have gone to Madhya Pradesh to the actual work site, but his boss was not talking about it at all.

Uttara came to Dharwad without knowing a word of Kannada. Though she had spent two years in Bangalore, one could live in the Institute without knowing the local language. Now, she wanted to learn Kannada as she had to converse with other people at home. She was yet to decide what she would do. Gopal was waiting for the next posting.

One day, Gopal told her, 'Uttara I have requested my company to post me to an area where we don't have projects that could lead to competition with your father's company. That will make us comfortable.'

'You are right, but our companies are competing in all the metro cities, except the North-east,' Uttara shrugged.

'My boss says, for a year or two we should be in the North-east, and later they will be able to post me to new projects in metros. What do you think?'

'You take it. A year will fly just like that.'

'But what work will you do in the North-east with your degree? There are no industries.'

'I will figure it out.'

Gopal and Uttara left for the North-east with plenty of enthusiasm.

Uttara found an engineering college which had just started a Computer Department. She joined as a lecturer. Although she had never taught anyone before, this stint turned out to be a fun experience. She enjoyed the leisure hours and became a very popular teacher. She never grumbled or talked about her education.

After two years, Gopal was posted to Mumbai after being promoted, and he was very happy.

Umesh got married. Uttara and Gopal went to the wedding, but they were not acknowledged by her family at all. It was a glamorous, expensive wedding at Ramoji Film City. Varieties of roses from all over India were ordered to decorate the venue for the day. Top-class musicians were called. Film stars were invited. But both of them felt out of place. She realized that she had to go back and insisted that Gopal leave immediately after the wedding ceremony. She felt it was nice to see such weddings from a distance, but never to be a part of them. It was hurtful for her to know that her family had almost forgotten her name.

Subbu too joined his work. He started observing people and gauged everyone—who among them was intelligent, who was gullible, who would be political and who was a loyalist. He knew that if you had to be successful, you needed a ladder. To start at the bottom of the ladder, you need a degree. To climb the ladder, you don't require any degree. You require shrewdness, a highly competitive self-centered motive and a sharp attitude. To go up the ladder, you must put your foot on someone's shoulder; it will be painful for that person, but you should not bother.

Subbu sourced information on Diwanji first and then on the company. Mr Diwanji was once upon a time a clerk in Gujarat and had understood the tactics and modus operandi of a good business. He had used this knowledge to climb the ladder and elevate his vision. Today, he was one of the billionaires. He had a lot of properties everywhere. Subbu's senior manager was Srikantaiah, a fellow Kannadiga from Mysore. He would make everyone work; take Subbu's work and show it to Diwanji as if it was his own, taking the opportunity of the fact that Subbu was a junior and may not be able to meet Diwanji. Subbu had patiently waited for a chance.

Sumithra felt that she knew very little of chemistry—given how vast it was. Though new girls had joined, she never felt the closeness that she had shared with Janaki and Uttara. At home, the situation was the same, but she had stopped worrying about it.

She would get emails from Uttara, Janaki and Arvind. She found Arvind's emails to be more informative. Sometimes, she would worry about what her future would be after her PhD. That time, she would remember Arvind who was like a philosopher and realized how difficult it would be to live like him.

Janaki was pressed for time in LA. She had rented a small house in which she lived with a housemate named Susan. Her friendship with Susan was very superficial which had set conditions such as no calls at night, no smoking and no staying with the boyfriend etc. It was strange but Janaki understood that this was the norm in America. She started pursuing her PhD.

A year passed. Suddenly, she received an email from Nakul—it came as a surprise to her.

He had written that he had secured admission to Stanford, a well-known university. However, he had to show a certain amount in his bank account to be able to process his visa.

He wanted to know if Janaki could help him in any way, in case he needed a backup.

Janaki felt it would be a good idea to help him. She was also bored without having any friends there.

She immediately agreed and gave him the required amount.

She never could have imagined how this sponsorship would change their lives.

Arvind started preparing to build rural houses. He used extensive computers and modern technology. He was supposed to meet his boss Mr Parekh, with whom he had never interacted before. When Arvind went for the meeting, Parekh had put both his legs on another chair and was smoking a cigar. Though there was another chair he did not have the courtesy to offer it to Arvind who started explaining the project. He realized that Parekh was not paying any attention. But Arvind continued, 'I got this type of knowledge when I studied at IISc, Bangalore.'

Immediately, Mr Parekh asked, 'Mr Shah, which mess did you go to? When my cousin was a student, I used to go there. I always ate in the south Indian mess. What great idli sambar they prepare.'

Mr Parekh's assistant, who was in the room, asked, 'Sir, that is the reason that you like the dahi vada even today?'

Mr Parekh continued talking about IISc, 'Which hostel were you staying in?'

With great disappointment, Arvind said, 'N-19.'

'Oh, my cousin stayed in M Block.'

His assistant asked, 'Sir how is IISc, according to you?'

'Oh, it is a great institute, but the food is better.'

Arvind lost his patience, 'No, sir. The food is great, but the institute is greater. Do you want me to continue?'

'No, for today it is more than enough. I must take my wife shopping,' said Mr Parekh as he got up.

Arvind was extremely upset with Mr Parekh and his irresponsible behaviour.

The assistant said again, 'Mr Shah, look at our boss. He cares so much for his family and his employees. He has a good work–life balance.'

After the assistant left, a senior arrived in the room and told Arvind, 'Mr Shah, when you get your salary, you should know that partially it is for your work, and most of it is given to spend and adjust with these lazy people.'

Arvind was surprised with the definition of salary in this company.

Gopal and Uttara reached Mumbai. The company gave them nice accommodation. By then, Uttara was able to adeptly handle money and cook well. She had learnt Kannada too. When she left the college in the North-east where she had taught, her students had cried. She felt that she had to do her PhD and become a full-time professor. However, it meant that she would have to leave Gopal for the next five years. It was hard for both of them.

She decided that she would take up a corporate job and started brushing up her knowledge for an interview. But on the day of the interview, she fell sick. When she went to the doctor, who, after examining her, said, 'Congratulations Mrs Rao, you are going to be a mother. But you have to take nine months of bed rest as your uterus is very weak.'

It was a moment of happiness and sadness—happiness because she was going to be a mother and sadness because she could not plan to work for the next year.

She had tears in her eyes. She was not very ambitious like Janaki, but she wanted to have a moderate career at least. However, the situation was against her, and she could not help it.

Srikantaiah would always stop Subbu when he wanted to design something new. 'Oh this is the new type,'

he would say, adding, 'Boss may not like it. Do it the old way.'

Subbu would smile and keep quiet.

He knew that the Goddess of success does not knock at your door twice and hence you should always keep the door open.

One day, Srikantaiah said, 'Today you make the best design and give it to me. I will discuss it with the boss and introduce you to him.' Subbu knew it was a lie.

That day, Diwanji was supposed to come to the office. Subbu designed and gave the file to Srikantaiah, just before the meeting.

When Diwanji was talking to Srikantaiah, he said, 'Sir I told you all the details and have done a new design.'

He was about to open the file and at that time, Subbu entered and said, 'Sir, you have forgotten to take the correct file. Here it is.' He presented the correct file to Diwanji himself. Srikantaiah was very upset.

Diwanji looked at the handsome young boy who was brimming with confidence. He thought for a moment and calculated something. When Srikantaiah was about to say something, Diwanji stopped him and instead asked Subbu, 'What is your name?'

'K. Subba Rao.'

'Where did you study?'

'Indian Institute of Science, Bangalore'

'Oh, then your designs may be new. Please show them to me.'

Happily, Subbu explained the details. Diwanji had a sharp mind and understood the process. 'Oh, bright people like you should not be here. You should be at the head office with me.' He turned to Srikantaiah and said, 'Make his relieving order. From tomorrow he will work with me.' Srikantaiah knew that no one could stop Subbu from climbing the ladder of success.

In that particular year, the company that Arvind worked for wanted to bring out a new calendar. Mr Parekh wanted a cut in that, so that he could pocket some money from the budget, and so he was choosing some low-quality photos. Arvind was arguing about the quality of work. He thought the best way to get Arvind out of this mess was to send him away for a week.

He said, 'Mr Shah, you are a technical man. Don't get involved in mundane work. There is a seminar on the latest technologies of this year at your own Institute in Bangalore. I think you should attend that. We will sponsor you.'

He turned to the assistant and said, 'Make all the necessary arrangements for his travel.' And without understanding his boss's intentions, Arvind was ready to go to Bangalore. But this time, he was forced to travel by plane owing to time constraints. Besides, Arvind was happy that he could meet Sumithra.

In Mumbai, Diwanji suffered a heart attack. He was bedridden for six weeks. That made Subbu in charge for all practical purposes. Now, even Srikantaiah had to report to him.

Subbu was required to go to Diwanji's house and take his signature on all required documents. During his first visit, Subbu saw that in a place like Mumbai, where cramped apartments are called paradise, Diwanji's villa stood mighty. It was on Nepean Sea Road and had many security guards outside. The house must have been around eighty years old with a chandelier, marble floor, an abundant garden, embroidered sofas and a swimming pool. Subbu felt it rather resembled a film set. In fact, it was bigger than Uttara's Lakshmi Niwas in Hyderabad and more affluent. Great pieces of artwork decorated the walls. Subbu did not know where to go. He stopped and sat on the sofa, waiting for someone to come and help him.

After some time, a beautiful young woman came down from the stairs. She was thin, seemed like she had bathed in perfume and was wearing an elegant dress. Without any expression, she said, 'I believe you are Mr Subba Rao and have come to meet my father. He has just gone to sleep. You have to wait till he wakes up. Do you want to have tea, coffee or juice?'

'No, water will do.'

She did not even insist and simply vanished upstairs.

A glass of water came with a helper, which Subbu had.

Lunch time passed but no lunch was offered to him.

Then, he got a call saying that Diwanji had woken up.

He took the boss' signature and went out. He turned back many times to get a glimpse of the woman but could not. In the next few weeks, Subbu would visit Diwanji at his house daily. Sometimes, the same lady would come and only when Diwanji said, she would offer him lunch on a silver plate.

Subbu had observed the woman—she had delicate features masked under too much make-up. He wanted to ask her many things—about her mother and siblings, but she would not encourage any conversation. She was reserved, and Subbu always felt she was like a lotus in a pond, meant only to be adored.

Uttara became a mother to a baby boy and named him Parikshit. She was unable to move throughout her pregnancy. Her mother never offered her any help. Instead, she let her mother-in-law take care. Sukanya came all the way to Mumbai to tend to her daughter-in-law. During Uttara's delivery, Kamakshi was abroad, and Uttara's sister Shamala's marriage was fixed with an NRI. Hence, she could not come. Her father sent her a congratulations card and a chain as a gift to the first grandchild. Though Uttara wanted to return it,

Gopal said, 'Don't do such things. Whatever said and done, he is their grandson.'

Her grandpa would call her every month and enquire about her and the child. He was very happy that he had a great-grandchild. He said, 'Actually they should do a Kanaka *abhisheka* for me, but nobody is interested.' Kanaka abhisheka is a ritual performed for great grandparents.

'Grandpa, if you come to Dharwad, we will do it in a big way. My mother-in-law is very keen on that. But such things will not happen in Hyderabad.'

Uttara remembered her grandpa's words, 'Uttara, when your child grows up, he should study at the Tata Institute.'

When Parikshit turned six months old, Uttara thought of taking up a job. But, Gopal got transferred to Delhi.

Arvind suddenly remembered that it was his father's birthday. He would not remember such occasions normally, but that day he felt like sending his father a card.

He wrote his address and put it in the office tray, for it to be sent by courier.

People hardly wrote letters in those days. However, Arvind's office maintained a courier tray. The old hog Sharma saw the address and called him inside the cabin. 'How are you Arvindji?' he asked with artificial affection.

'I am as usual. Nothing special.'

'You never tell anything about your personal life.'

'Why should I tell you? It is not a part of my job.'

'You should have told me that you are the son of Chandmalji of Beespur.'

'How did you come to know? That is my personal letter. Why did you see that?' Arvind was a little uncomfortable.

'Oh, by mistake,' he said with a wicked smile and continued, 'You are such a rich man's son. Why are you working here?'

'I like to work,' Arvind said and went away.

From that day onwards, Mr Parekh and Sharma started respecting Arvind.

A few months passed. Arvind was going through the budget and came across an error.

He went to Sharma and said, 'Your quotes are wrong.'

'No. We are very experienced people.'

Sharma wanted to close the topic.

'No. I checked it twice. You have doubled it.'

'How do you believe computers so much. After all, it is a machine. It can make mistakes.'

'No. You cannot talk about computers like that. I understand what you have been up to now. You buy low-quality cement at a cheap rate and produce false receipts, build bridges and houses with that. They could collapse and many people will die because of your injustice.'

'No, such things have not happened in our company. And suppose something like that does happen, then you should take it lightly and think the population has decreased.'

Arvind stood up because of the foolish joke and said, 'This is not the way to reduce population, and you cannot be so unfair at your job. Maybe I should inform this to the press.'

He said this as he lacked faith that Mr Parekh would take this forward.

Sharmaji was now worried, 'No, don't do that. Come to Mr Parekh's office and we will discuss this.'

In Mr Parekh's cabin, both Mr Parekh and Sharma were deep in discussion. Arvind was sitting outside, biting his nails.

He thought that there might be many companies like this in India, which have been cheating poor people. He felt bad for being a part of such a company. Unable to contain himself, he walked inside Mr Parekh's cabin.

'Mr Parekh, you are doing wrong things,' he said.

'Mr Shah, you are not aware about how a business runs, where we have to take care of all the people who are involved?'

'Why do you need to take care of so many people?'

'If we do not generate profit . . . ours is a public limited company and shareholders will raise objections. We will lose our heads.'

'Please educate our shareholders,' Arvind pleaded.

'Mr Shah, for your kind information, the majority of the shares of this company are held by Chandmalji of Beespur. You can go and educate them, not us. We will also be happy. Will they listen to you? No, they will not. In this life, you hardly meet someone who does not bow down his head in front of money.'

Arvind was stunned and asked for a pen.

He took out a piece of white paper, scribbled something and gave it to Parekh.

'What is this?' Parekh asked.

'My resignation,' Arvind said. He walked out of the cabin without waiting for a response.

Arvind received an email from Sumithra when he reached his barsati. It felt like a spring of fresh cold water in hot summer. The email contained information of his interest.

'I met Prof. Parameshwaran at Coimbatore, to present a paper. Mr Parameshwaran works for the tribal people, and he is a retired professor. He wants someone like you to give new ideas. They have received funding from the United Nations. So, I consider that it might be a good opportunity for you. Please go and discuss the terms and conditions with him. Right now, he is working in Madhya Pradesh.'

Arvind immediately called Prof. Parameshwaran and established the link. They found each other to be like-minded.

However, this time around, Arvind was a little cautious.

'I will work for six months and if both of us are happy, then we will think about the future development,' he said.

Sumithra finally finished her thesis and was very happy. However, she did not know what she had to do next or where she could pursue her post-doctoral degree. The dilemma persisted—should she go abroad, or should she take up a job? Her mind remained divided for a while.

After some deliberation, Sumithra decided that she would work abroad for a few years and then think it over. She bagged a scholarship from a prestigious German university. At home, her parents knew that there was no hope for her marriage, and so they did not stop her. And, as she had been away from home during the last few years, she did not bother about the opinion of the old people at home. She knew that she was the captain of her life-ship. So, she packed her luggage and moved to Germany.

Janaki and Nakul finished their degrees at UCLA and Stanford, respectively. She joined Google and he, IBM. Though their offices were in San Francisco, both were posted in Los Angeles. She would visit San Francisco once a month to meet her bosses. She was smart in her work, had joined earlier than Nakul and so, she progressed sooner than him. Yet, her mind was not at peace. Ultimately, she wanted to start her own company. But, for that, she would require a few years of experience, an understanding of the industry, networking with angel investors and raising funds.

Her parents would often call her and ask, 'Janaki, are you coming to India? If you are settling in America, then find a partner. We want you to get married. You have the freedom to choose a boy from any country. We don't have any objection. We are getting old, and we want to see grandchildren.'

Meera once told her daughter, 'A woman's window for marriage and conceiving a child is limited. It will not wait. Don't you know that time and tide wait for no one? You are fond of children. Please think about your marriage seriously. If you want to

153

marry a Maharashtrian, then register on one of the Indian marriage websites. We don't know any eligible bachelors in America or India, who will be up to your standard.'

None of these talks affected Janaki. She had seen people getting married later in life and having children, thanks to advanced medical science. Just because she liked children, did not mean she should have immediately. Checking the profile of grooms in the Marathi section of the marriage bureau website was unimaginable for a person like Janaki. Despite being a Maharashtrian, she had only once or twice visited the Maharashtra Mandal in America. Nothing about it fascinated her.

Even while pursuing her PhD, she had met many boys—but they all had girlfriends. They had wondered how Janaki was single even at this age, in America. But she did not care about people's opinions. Once Nakul shifted to Los Angeles, they stayed in the same neighbourhood and often met as friends. Some people mistook Nakul to be Janaki's boyfriend. She was friendly with Nakul for various reasons. He brought a sense of familiarity and was a good man. But marriage, according to her, required something more than that. She was not like Uttara—emotional or someone who would put her career at stake.

Janaki desired a man who could understand and help her achieve her ambition. She could have discussed this with Nakul, but something held her back. She didn't want him to mistake her talk for something else, because she had helped him to come to the US. That evening she received a call from Nakul, asking her to meet at Sun and Sand Restaurant on Santa Monica beach. She agreed since it was the weekend.

However, she could not help but wonder why he had called her to a restaurant. Normally, he would just drop by her home—a nice apartment given by the company, opposite a seashore. One could see the white sand of Santa Monica. Her parents had come once to stay with her briefly. They enjoyed the serenity of the neighbourhood and the long walks on the beach. But within two months, they had returned to crowded Shreyas Apartments in Pune.

She was so immersed in her work that she hardly took walks, though people from other localities came and parked their cars before embarking on leisurely strolls. It was one of the coveted places in Los Angeles city.

When she went to the restaurant, Nakul was not there. She waited for him. Her mind wandered to the children playing on the seashore and their mothers running behind them. She felt it was nice to have children but also felt that it was like having an additional job. *All these mothers must have sacrificed a lot for their children, as in this country, they don't get much domestic help to raise the children,* she thought.

She hadn't noticed Nakul walking in and sitting at her table.

'Hi Jani, what's up?'

'Nakul, I was just thinking about starting my own company and entrepreneurship. It is not hard but requires tremendous dedication and hard work.'

'Yes, I agree Jani. I have observed many youngsters in the Bay area. Particularly new entrepreneurs. How they work and travel. What sacrifices do they make to build a company. They are not present for their wives or children. I feel, behind every entrepreneur, there is an understanding person, who allows them to enjoy all the comforts without any responsibility.'

Janaki added, 'Maybe for men, it is easy. Their wives are supportive. But for women, it is very difficult. There are very few men who stand by her, support her every venture and take the brunt that comes with her entrepreneurship. Then only can she succeed. Otherwise, she should remain unmarried. It is of course unfair to her.'

'Jani, if you wholeheartedly agree, as your husband I will be the person who will help you to build that company. I liked you the day you came to our house in Bangalore several years back. I have always appreciated you. But I have never expressed it before because I was a little hesitant. Now, I feel I must tell you.'

A happily surprised Janaki smiled at him, 'How do you know what is running in my mind.'

'Because I am your mind.'

Soon, the news of Nakul and Janaki getting married reached all of their friends.

Uttara was in no position to attend the wedding. This time, with great difficulty, she had conceived a second time and was advised nine months' bedrest like the last time.

When they discussed the second child, Gopal was unhappy.

'At what cost do you want the second child, Uttara? It will affect your health and career. I feel sad that you are so intelligent and are not focusing on your career. Think it over. One child is more than enough. We can always adopt one more child, the way my parents did.'

'No, I want to have one more child, a nice sibling for Parikshit. And yes, maybe we will adopt one more child, like your parents did. The best ever gift we can give our children in their childhood is siblings. Even when we are not there, siblings will care for each other. I am ready to undergo the physical pain and loss of my career for this wish.'

Gopal would never go against her wish. He was always in awe of her personality and her affection. He had seen no one adapt as Uttara did.

In such a situation, they could not fly to America for a wedding.

Arvind was not the type who would fly to America for a wedding. He never attended his own cousins' weddings in India, forget going to America. He just sent an e-greeting and forgot about it.

Sumithra was in the US for a seminar, but at the wedding time, she had come to India as one of her grand-aunts had passed away.

Subbu was busy with his own games and attending the wedding was not a part of that.

Diwanji had a textile industry in Pune. Its CEO had just resigned and left. So, Diwanji had requested Subbu to be there for some time until he brought in a new CEO. Subbu went to Pune. He never wanted to stay in a guest house because he felt everyone would observe his movements and report incorrectly to the top. Therefore, he stayed in a furnished apartment. He had lots of acquaintances in Pune and could meet them often.

The work was not so much compared to the Mumbai office. So, he could undertake several personal tasks. He would send his new visiting cards with his designation prominent—general manager, operations—to all his contacts. He changed his address database to remove the names which were less important and added influential people. He had saved a lot of money, and by doing so, he had fulfilled his mother's desire. His parents had left the rented house and had purchased a prime property in Malleshwaram in Bangalore. His sister Mangala's marriage was also fixed. Given his position as the general manager, good alliances had come for Mangala. She was no longer the daughter of a postman. His brother Diwakar had joined a CA course.

In Pune, Subbu had an old personal assistant, who would greet him with a namaskar all the time. Subbu thought that perhaps it was a part of the factory's culture. After two weeks, one day in his office, he wanted to dictate a letter and pressed the bell. The personal assistant came. It stunned Subbu as it was a young woman in her early twenties instead of the old man. She was thin and tall, had no make-up on, and was wearing a simple cotton saree and a few glass bangles. She was more beautiful than any film actress. He could see her beautiful features and enthusiasm on her face. Her eyes were bright and big. Young Subbu kept on looking at her and forgot his work. She had a dimpled chin and Subbu fell for it immediately.

Without realizing that Subbu was smitten, she smiled and said, 'Good morning, sir. My name is Sarala. I am your personal assistant. I was on leave for the last two weeks.'

The next day onwards, Subbu's working style changed. He would call her without any reason so that he could talk to her.

Subbu verified her background—she was from an extremely underprivileged family from Jamakhandi. Her father was a security personnel. She had two sisters, who were studying in Jamakhandi. Sarala had completed her secretarial course from a government polytechnic and was a rank holder. With her college reference, she had come to Pune for the job and stayed at a working women's hostel. She was her family's main breadwinner.

Sarala was attracted to Subbu too. After all, he was a handsome and young boss. Subbu was attracted to her beauty. It is natural to be drawn to the opposite gender at a young age. Moths are attracted to the light of the fire, but they are often unaware that it could burn them.

Arvind got the opportunity to visit Haripur in Madhya Pradesh for his project. There were many villages—in one of those, his new employer, Prof. Parameshwaran, stayed with his wife Rukmini. He was a man in his sixties, very mature and he understood human nature. He welcomed Arvind and made him feel at home.

He and his wife stayed in a very modest house. They had a jeep and a cycle to travel. Electricity and water were a luxury there. For Wi-Fi or internet, they had to walk a couple of miles, closer to the tower.

Their house was located around a moderately thick forest of mahua and bamboo trees. Many tribal people lived in the *basti*s around the jungle, with their community growing what they needed, like wheat, rice, turmeric and chillies. They also reared cattle.

Some of the locals were good at painting, sculpting, etc. There was a school, but it was not well equipped, had a poor approach to discipline and the children hardly attended it.

After dinner, Prof. Parameshwaran and Arvind got to know each other. Prof. Parameshwaran was the first to elaborate on his background. He said, 'I have taught at the IIT. Both my children have done well with education and are settled abroad; they have married Indian girls. I requested them to return to India, work here and help people. One of them is a doctor. I requested him, saying that the fee for a seat earned on merit in a medical college is low in India. It has been subsidized by taxpayers' money. And that he owes our country a lot. Take education, learn new things but come back to India. The other one is a civil engineer from IIT. He also did the same.'

'Why have they not come back?'

'It is very simple,' said Rukmini.

'My daughters-in-law have a free life there. They feel they might be restricted if they come here. Though I don't interfere, they feel I am watching them. They don't want to take responsibility for older people. We may go and stay for a few months in a year, with them. But they do not want to live with us forever.'

Prof. Parameshwaran smiled and said, 'That may be one of the reasons, but the real reason is they love money and luxury. They are attracted to that life. Sometimes, I wonder where I went wrong. I have failed to impart good values. I do not know what it is. Perhaps it is peer pressure, but children change once they go abroad.'

'Then, why are you here?' Arvind bluntly asked.

'I have always wanted to work for poor people. After my early retirement, I decided that as long as my health is good, I will work in a domain where nobody works. I came from a poor family in rural Andhra, and I know what it is like to be in a village with fewer facilities.

'So, I decided to take this job. I have my pension, so there is no worry. I do attend some seminars and have good connections at the UN that help me secure funding for the projects. Money is not the problem. The problem is getting passionate people.

'When Dr Sumithra spoke about you, I wanted you to come and see this place. I will pay you a reasonably good salary; however, it may not be the market standard.

'You may try working for a few months. If you do not like it, you may go back. I will not harbour any ill feelings.

'Many people have come here, but only to return within a few months. You might feel intellectually lonely, the work might not progress quickly, and you might not get glory. Because there is no glamour in this. You will be unsung. In a worldly way, there is no incentive to work here. But if you are passionate, this will be the best place to work. I will give you another hut like mine, with minimum facilities. We have many volunteers here and they can help you and explain,' Prof. Parmeshwaram said.

'I will work for a few days and decide,' said Arvind.

'I was wondering how a bright boy like you, who has an ME in civil, can help this village!' said Prof. Parmeshwaram.

'I have some ideas about rural development. I want to try them out. But theory is different than practice. As long as I have a free hand and transparency in the work, I will not have any problem.'

Sumithra published many international papers and wrote a book on chemistry. It became a bestseller in that field and people started noticing her. She became one of the coveted speakers at academic events. One day, she saw that IISc had advertised to fill the post of a professor. Sumithra felt that this was the best time for her to relocate. By this time, she had a tenured professorship in the US, but somehow, she felt that it was best for her to move back to India. Many of her professors advised her that it was unwise to move away as she would miss many opportunities.

But she was adamant. 'Due to computers and the internet, the world has become small. People are global citizens. I will work from India; it does not matter,' she said to all the naysayers.

She secured the job at IISc and moved into the Institute's staff accommodation. Whenever she would walk past the girls' hostel, the Automation Department, lecture halls and the library, she remembered all her good friends.

Janaki and Nakul had a court wedding in the US, followed by a reception for local friends. The Paranjapes were happy, but the Aptes weren't. They felt they could have got a better, homely girl, who would depend on Nakul and not the business-oriented Janaki.

Sushila Apte was unhappy for various reasons. She said to herself, 'I wish Nakul had chosen a younger girl, not someone of the same age. There were so many beautiful girls in our own community. I do not know what he liked in Janaki.'

Despite their inhibitions, they came for the wedding as per the customs.

The Paranjapes requested Janaki and Nakul to agree for a small reception in Pune, for the sake of their friends. However, Janaki said, 'It is just not possible for the next two years. Both of us are very busy.' Marriage did not affect Janaki and Nakul's life much, except that Nakul shifted to Janaki's house.

She would go about her routine like before. She had hired a Gujarati cook, who would prepare food and refrigerate it. There was a lady to clean the house and do laundry twice a week.

With Nakul's assurance, she felt relieved, and so, she started preparing to establish her own company. Nakul would travel on and off for his work, but it did not bother Janaki much.

Subbu grew more attracted to Sarala with every passing day. He was aware that other people had noticed his behaviour. So, he could not spend much time with her. But he would feel very energetic in her company. But now, the only way he could see her was outside the office. Thus, he took the risk of asking Sarala out, despite the initial hesitation. One day when she came into his room with her writing pad, he asked, 'Sarala, have you seen Lonavala?'

'No, sir. Not yet.'

'Will you come?'

'Who all?'

Subbu thought for a minute and said to himself: *Let me be open with her. At the most, she will decline.*

'No one, just you and me,' he said.

Sarala was scared for a moment. He could read her face. She asked, 'Why in this rainy season?'

'Lonavala looks beautiful during the monsoon,' he said, paused and continued, 'I want the answer. I am not insisting. You are an adult. But, on Saturday morning I will wait for you at Aundh. We can drive from there.'

'Can we be back by evening?'

'Maybe,' Subbu smiled. He knew for sure she would come.

Sarala was worried. *Is it all right to be with a man before marriage?* she thought.

In office, everybody would say that Subba Rao was an eligible bachelor. Some senior employees were trying to get their daughters' proposals to him, but Sarala knew she was the most beautiful of them all. Her beauty was her asset, and she knew that Subbu was enchanted by her and eventually, they could marry.

A girl with no exposure to the modern world and corporate life believed Subbu and assumed he would propose to her one day.

On Saturday morning, it was drizzling and was very cold.

Sarala was waiting with anxiety. It would be her first car drive with a young man. The green bangles on her slender wrists were jingling pleasantly. The jasmine in her hair was enchanting. When Subbu saw her, he felt that all the photos of the prospective brides that Gowramma had sent him paled in comparison to Sarala.

They reached Lonavala and the rains became heavier. Subbu knew where to stay. He had booked an old bungalow, on the top of a hill. When they went in, the *chowkidar* looked at them. He deemed them to be a normal couple and did not bother.

By the time they got out of the car and went to the portico, a part of her saree was drenched. There was nobody in the bungalow. This was the first time that Subbu touched Sarala's hands. He said, 'Sarala, I love you.' The doors closed.

Arvind was enjoying his work in Haripur. He felt that he had reached the right place and finally had the right mentor. Sumithra's emails always encouraged him to work. She once wrote, 'You are a very unusual person, born to change people, make a mark in the country. I am very proud that you are my friend.'

Janaki told him over email, 'Arvind, if you are doing any project regarding the welfare of women, let me know. I would like to fund it.'

Uttara wrote, 'You need a break from your work. In winter, Gopal will be working in Bhopal for two months. Our family will come there. Why don't you visit us?'

But Subbu always looked down upon Arvind, thinking he was wasting his talent in a village. He never bothered getting in touch with him.

In Beespur, Arvind's family was very upset with him. 'What is he doing? If he had to do social work, why did he go to IIT and IISc? It does not require any intelligence. He could have done without schooling.'

Arvind ignored those comments.

Meanwhile, Subbu's Lonavala trips continued for some time. Sarala had accepted Subbu as her husband in her mind. She daydreamt about her family and their yet-to-be-born children. He had got her beautiful earrings, a necklace and branded clothes. Her dress sense and etiquette had received an upgrade. A few days later, she insisted that he meet her father. 'As I have promised you, I have not shared this with anybody,' she said.

'Yes, Sarala, even I have not told anyone, including my mother, though I am very close to her. This weekend I am going to Bangalore. I will speak to her and then I will come to your house. We will surprise everyone.'

Sarala was on cloud nine.

That Friday, Subbu got a call from Diwanji calling him to Mumbai immediately. By Saturday morning, he was in Diwanji's villa for breakfast. By now, he was a familiar sight in their home.

Diwanji himself welcomed him.

'Subbu, how is the work in Pune?' he asked.

'Very nice, sir. I am enjoying it,' Subbu said and smiled.

He called his daughter, Veena, and said, 'Please arrange breakfast. We will be there in five minutes.'

Subbu looked at Veena. She appeared rather fake to him with her make-up and real jewellery. He remembered Sarala and her simplicity and was proud of having found her.

Diwanji said, 'Subbu, I want to ask you a personal thing. No obligation. Will you marry my daughter Veena?'

'Excuse me, sir?' Subbu was unable to believe these words.

'Yes, Subbu, I wanted to know if you would marry my daughter. I know, our communities, backgrounds and languages are different. Both of you were brought up differently. But I know that it is possible to adjust because I am from a poor family and Veena's mother was from a rich family. This house is Veena's mother's, given to us at our wedding.'

Subbu was searching for an appropriate response.

Diwanji continued, 'I want Veena to marry a bright young boy, and she is my only daughter. The man should not marry her for money but should be invested in his work, and you are that kind of a person.'

'What is Veena's opinion, sir?'

'I have taken her consent and only then did I approach you.'

Just then, he received a call from London. He left the room to attend it, leaving Subbu alone. He had to make a life-changing decision within the next few minutes.

On one side of the scale, there was Sarala, and on the other side was Veena.

If he married Sarala, what would he get? A beautiful Sarala, dependent on him, and her family who would gain from this marriage, including the responsibilities of her two sisters. If he married Veena, what would he gain? She was not bad looking, she would come with money, position, status and honour—everything that he had longed for, for a long time. His dream would be realized with not much effort on his end.

Suppose he declined the offer. He thought that there was a chance that Diwanji might transfer him, take back his position or marry Veena off to someone who would eventually be his boss.

He felt bad for Sarala, but his mind said she was an adult, and she knew what she was doing.

By that time, Diwanji returned and asked, 'So Subbu, what did you decide?'

He added, 'If you agree, we will go to Bangalore on our plane and meet your parents.'

Diwanji knew how to read someone's mind very well. That was the reason behind his success over the last five decades. Whether the call was from London or not, he purposely left Subbu to think for a few minutes. He almost knew what the result would be.

'Sir, will I really be so fortunate to be your son-in-law?'

In the balance of life, Veena weighed heavier than Sarala.

The news quickly spread in the office.

When the engagement card reached all senior staff, Sarala could not believe her eyes. She was unable to bear the agony. The castle of her dreams came crashing down, and she started choking on her tears. Her heartbeat increased. Looking at her condition, her senior colleague, Mrs Deshpande, asked, 'Are you okay, Sarala? Anything wrong?'

'Yesterday, I was on fast and so am feeling giddy,' she said.

'Then you apply for half-day leave, go home and rest,' she advised.

Sarala was unable to understand how things could change within two days. She had loved Subbu wholeheartedly. He had taken advantage of her innocence, she realized.

The fault lies with me. Why would a handsome and successful man fall for me? It only happens in the movies. And why did I like him so much? Why did I go out of the way to make him happy? Because I also fell into the greed of marrying a rich man. I wanted to escape my poverty.

The day before, her father had sent Sarala's proposal to a clerk in the school in Pune, and according to him, it was a big match. She had looked down upon that groom. Now, she did not have any other choice but to say yes.

For a minute, she felt she should write a letter to Subbu but did not have the courage. If the news of this affair spreads, she would remain unmarried and bring a bad name to the family.

Her sisters would not get married either. She may stay jobless, so it was best for her to swallow her sorrow. She asked God, 'Is there any justice in your kingdom?' She cried continuously.

It was the death of love. God's justice would come later, unbeknownst to her.

That winter, Gopal visited Bhopal for his work. He was now one of the directors of Dinshaw. The company had done very well over the years, and the management had come to consider Gopal as an asset. He had all the privileges like that of an owner.

During this time, he also witnessed the unfortunate slow fall of Venkateshwara Rao's company. There was a quarrel between Shamala's NRI husband, who claimed Shamala's share in property, and Umesh, who was the head of the company. The friction started among the men, and the women got involved eventually. The three women in the family did not get along at all. Kamakshi was always upset with her daughter and daughter-in-law and vice versa. Vekateshwara Rao's company suffered amid the fights. They had to liquidate a lot of their assets.

People who knew that Gopal was the first son-in-law of the house, provided him with inside information. He refrained from passing it on to Uttara, because he knew that it would spoil her mood. Any woman wishes the best for her maternal home and prays for its prosperity and Uttara was no exception.

Uttara was sad for she had hardly visited Hyderabad of late. During her last visit, she had been able to assess the situation and could not stay on any longer. She felt sorry for her grandpa whom she loved immensely. When Gopal asked the reason behind her sadness, Uttara said, 'My grandpa is old, and nobody bothers about him. He has transferred all his assets to my father and brother. So, he has become irrelevant. Would you mind bringing him to our house for a few days?'

'You don't have to ask me Uttara, this is your house. I am not that fortunate to have a grandfather. Please bring him.'

Rama Rao came to Uttara's place and felt very satisfied on seeing how happy Uttara and Gopal were with each other. He thanked God that his granddaughter was so blessed to have such a good family life. He did feel sad that Uttara had not made her career. Instead, she was now teaching at a local college. She had not made the best use of her IISc degree.

But to get something, you must lose something. That is a part of life.

Meanwhile, Uttara had arranged to meet with Sumithra and Arvind. 'We will be in Bhopal for a month. Please do come and spend some time. I will take you to Sanchi to see the great *stupa* of Ashoka.'

Arvind agreed immediately.

Arvind had visited his home in Beespur on very few occasions over the last few years. Of late, Chandmalji was not keeping good health and had forgotten about Arvind's marriage. He had written his will, keeping most of his assets for his first two children, Suraj and Ramesh, and some money in Arvind's name.

'By mistake, Arvind was born into our family. Nowadays, I believe in karma and rebirth. So maybe he was born for some reason, maybe to fulfil his incomplete wishes from a past life. Don't use harsh words on him. He has an entirely different personality. Help him when he needs it. Forgive his mistakes and treat him like your son,' Chandmalji said to Arvind's brothers.

Suraj and Ramesh also had grown apart and had their own separate houses. The relations between the daughters-in-law improved after the assets were separated.

Chandmalji continued to stay in the old house with his sisters.

Once, when Arvind was visiting his father, he said, 'Baba, throughout your life, you have worked for money and have made good assets for your children.

But you have neglected yourself. I have seen that people of your age in Haripur are still active. They smile, they walk, they do all their work. They do have some difficulties. But by and large, they enjoy their life. Baba, if you agree, I want to take you there. Money has not brought you health.'

Chandmalji agreed partially but did not venture out immediately.

When Sumithra received the invitation to visit Bhopal, her secretary called the Department of Chemistry in the University of Bhopal. They were elated and invited Sumithra for a lecture. The number of papers she had written was phenomenal. That year, she published another book and was appointed Fellow of the Royal Society, London. It was obvious that her lecture would be a matter of privilege in any university. Arvind was very happy. Of all the friends, she was the closest to him, but they were unable to meet often because of their busy lives. They would get on to Zoom calls whenever time and internet speed permitted. He also wanted to meet Uttara. So, they all met after many years.

Sumithra came by flight. Uttara went to the airport to receive her. However, Sumithra insisted that she would spend a day with them, but she would stay at the campus. Many students visited her. Arvind came by train and reached Uttara's home on his own.

Sumithra said, 'Uttara, you look like a middle-aged person. You have put on weight.'

'Of course, I am a mother of two children. Sumi, you have grey hair?'

'Yes, I am a mother of two books!'

They both laughed.

Arvind came home. He looked almost the same. Uttara made fun of him, 'Arvind, you are working with tribals. So, you must have some concoction to stay young!'

'Not at all. I enjoy my work and that keeps me young.'

'That is not true, Arvind. I also enjoy my work, but I have grown old.'

'Uttara is right. You must be having some medicine or fruit or seed to remain young!'

Everybody was overjoyed after seeing Uttara's happy home. Sumithra noticed that even after many years of marriage, Gopal and Uttara cared about each other the same way they did when they were young. Time had not touched their relationship negatively. She thought Uttara was very blessed.

After Sumithra's lecture, all of them went to see Arvind's work in this village. He had created simple toys, meaningful scientific experiments and connected the artisans to the market. The children were extremely happy to see the forest, school, weaving machines, the singing and the dancing.

Gopal and others truly felt the mark Arvind had made on these people's lives. They also met Prof. Parameshwaran and his wife.

Sumithra and Gopal went with the children. Uttara and Arvind were alone, discussing work.

Prof. Parameshwaran and his wife were very happy to see the children and the guests. They longed a lot for grandchildren, but their own grandchildren would never visit this village. More than that, their sons and daughters-in-law believed that this was an unsafe place—and that it was infested with mosquitoes, had no clean water or medical aid and so on. Once they had bluntly said, 'If you want to meet your grandchildren, come to Hyderabad. We can all stay at a five-star hotel. You can spend a week with them. But definitely not at Haripur.'

They did go to Hyderabad a couple of times, but there was so much disconnect. When the children grew up, they preferred to spend their vacation in Europe, rather than in India.

Prof. Parameshwaran and his wife saw Sumithra and Arvind walking with the children, towards the tribal area, and Gopal and Uttara were happily talking under a tree shade.

Rukmini commented, 'Don't you think it is high time for Arvind to have a life companion! It will be so nice. Anyway, he has known Sumithra for a long time. They have been classmates. Will it not be a good idea to marry someone like her?'

The professor laughed and said, 'What a foolish idea you have! She is a scholar, immersed in her chemistry. Just because they are friends, it does not mean they can marry. Her aspirations and area of expertise are different from his. They may visit each other but don't expect such a bride for Arvind.'

'What happens if he marries a traditional girl from Beespur?'

'She won't stay here for more than three months. Their lifestyles are so different.'

'Then whom should he marry?'

'Someone like you, who believes in her husband, confidently follows him, enjoys and helps his work.'

Rukmini blushed.

Subbu's marriage was a big event. Most of his guests had come in private planes. Some called this Indira's *darbar*. But Gowramma was a little concerned.

'Subbu, they are too rich. I don't know their language. How will I communicate with my daughter-in-law?'

'What do you want to communicate?'

'I want to tell her our customs, Gowri Ganesha, Varamahalakshmi, Navaratri and much more.'

Subbu laughed at his mother's expectations. He knew Veena would not do any of this. He also remembered Uttara who would follow all customs at her in-laws. Once, when they lived in Mumbai, she had called him for Bombe Habba. Subbu remembered participating in the festival as a kid in his neighbourhood. They used to give different kinds of prasad every day. But not everybody was Uttara. Though Veena and Uttara came from similar backgrounds, their mindsets were so different. Veena was from the cosmopolitan Mumbai whereas Uttara was from a proper south Indian city.

He was not able to explain this to his mother. He knew that his mother would not understand, and neither could he explain to Veena.

Gowramma purchased a contrast-border Mysore silk sari and south Indian-style *mangalasutra* for her daughter-in-law. But Veena did not even look at them. Her wardrobe was full of *zardozi* lehengas, chiffon saris which were dazzling with crystals. Tribhuvan Das Zaveri, a well-known jeweller from Mumbai, had customized her jewellery for the wedding.

She had softly but firmly told her mother-in-law, 'My designer says this sari and jewellery do not match my style.' Gowramma did not understand this at all.

Veena took charge of planning their honeymoon. The destination was Paris. Veena had seen Paris many times before but for Subbu, it was the first time.

Subbu was fascinated by the city, whereas Veena was taken by the variety of perfumes. After dinner, Veena ordered drinks. It was a surprise to Subbu as Diwanji was very traditional.

He looked at her and said, 'I don't drink.'

'Is it? I am surprised. In my circle everybody does. It is only a social drink. Come on Subbu, take a sip.'

Subbu's middle-class values did not allow him to partake in the drinking. He wondered what was considered normal in Veena's circle and was thinking about what else was in store for him.

As per his habit, Subbu started assessing Veena.

Though he had met her many times before marriage, he had been unable to do it. Veena was not a bad girl, but she did not have her strength, her own identity. She was not shrewd like her father and was stubborn and headstrong. Veena never thought deeply about anything in life. She held her father in high regard. He was everything to her.

Subbu wanted a small reception in Bangalore as that was the only thing Gowramma had asked for, but Veena had rejected it, saying, 'Oh, I do not like too many ceremonies.'

Subbu could not argue with her. One day, he was having vangibath prepared by his mother at their Bangalore home. He loved it and said, 'Amma, it is excellent. No seven-star chef can prepare it like this.'

Subbu was genuine in his praise.

A mother's affection makes for the perfect cooking ingredient, making every dish lovely, thought Gowramma.

Then she gave a piece of paper with something scribbled on it to Subbu. 'Subbu, I do not know English, I have written how to prepare vangibath powder in Kannada. Please read it to your wife and note down this recipe in English. Don't go on YouTube for this. This is our family's traditional recipe. Tell Veena to cook for you or she can ask your cook to prepare for you.' Subbu smiled and took the paper. By this time, he knew how his wife was, and he dropped the paper in the dustbin at the airport.

Janaki had been married for some time now and had started her own company.

But in a way, she still felt that she was not yet established.

For the first two years, she did not worry about having children. Now, she was thinking about it—she felt it was the right time to have a child. Nakul and Janaki tried but she was unable to conceive. She met a specialist eventually. The doctor said, 'Of late, natural conception has become very uncommon. IVF is preferred. You should go for it.'

Janaki accepted it because by the time she had researched IVF on the internet. Nakul agreed to it too. Still, she did not conceive.

She always believed that America was the land of advancement, and her age would not matter there. She was under the impression that advanced treatment would always help her. She had also seen people having a child even after forty. But the doctor said, 'Even as we try our level best, it also differs from one genetic make-up to another, from one race to another. But there is some unknown factor which is beyond our explanation. Let us see. We will give you a supplement.'

Disappointed, Janaki went for an alternate treatment.

Meanwhile, professionally, Nakul worked very hard but still, he was unable to match Janaki's level be it in terms of putting in the hard work or professional achievements. He was a let-go type of person. As he believed that there was much to see in America, he wanted to spend every weekend outdoors.

He supported Janaki's projects, but she would work even on the weekends. 'Nakul, if you want you can go anywhere. I will not stop you, but I will not come until my company is well established.'

Nakul was disappointed. He felt life had become routine and boring.

There was no change at home at all. Due to her hectic schedule, Janaki would not host any guests but had told Nakul that he could do it. Initially, he did that, but later that was also boring for him.

His friends came with their wives and ultimately, would end up discussing children. They talked about doctors, the best schools, daycare and holiday sites. Nakul would feel like an odd man out.

After some time, he stopped entertaining guests. He was upset about his life.

All his cousins in India had a better life, he felt. They were with parents, celebrating festivals and amid their own culture. He felt the stark contrast of culture in America.

He felt they should return to India, but he knew that Janaki would never agree. He also knew Janaki's loyalty towards him. As soon as she came home, she would cook what he might like—she managed the kitchen throughout the week. But she had limited time.

He was also disappointed with the delay in conceiving the child.

One day Janaki brought a bittersweet piece of news. On a happy note, she had bagged a very good client, and the sad part was that he was in Boston, where she would have to spend the next six months. Nakul was not happy. He said, 'Leave this contract, you can get another one. But I really feel you should not go to Boston for six months. I will get bored here.'

'Nakul, entrepreneurs undergo all these difficulties initially. Once they overcome it, it will be easy. Subsequently, I will certainly not do this. But now it is a good break for me to establish myself and get visibility. Now, if I choose family over this work, then I will never become an entrepreneur. I will remain an ordinary person.'

'Oh. You mean to say like me?'

'No. I never said that. Why do you think that way?'

'Janaki, now I think you should concentrate on our family. See how Uttara manages her family. Priorities should change with age.'

Janaki removed her specs and said, 'I am different from Uttara. And I know her pain for dropping her career. I will never do it. I don't want to regret anything in life. If you feel lonely, you can call your parents or find a hobby that keeps you busy. But you cannot tell me to quit my career. I don't have any incentive to stay at home. I am not used to sitting at home either.'

Affectionately, she continued, 'I will come from Boston every Friday. I will take a red-eye flight on

Sunday and return. We will spend the weekend together. If my work goes well, I will request them to release me early. Nakul, let us walk through this difficult patch together for six months. And I promise I will not take any such assignments in future.'

Nakul did not reply.

On Monday morning, he discovered that he was assigned a new executive assistant at his office.

She was a talkative young girl in her early twenties, who had just finished her degree and had come for an internship, which she had to complete in the final semester. She was a fun-loving, happy-go-lucky, beautiful Indian girl.

After meeting him over just one day, she shared everything about herself with Nakul.

She was born and brought up in Ohio under strict parentage. That made her slightly rebellious—it showed when she changed her name from Saraswati to Sara. She wanted to be away from her parents, so she chose sunny California.

She never learnt any Indian language. She just did not like to be identified with Indians. She preferred to speak French, Spanish or English.

After a few weeks, Nakul became very close to her and developed an attraction. He always enjoyed her company. He would take her out for lunch, and she would not fuss. That night Nakul reflected on Janaki. She was like a teacher whom you were afraid of and respected. But Sara was young and fun. She was like a breath of fresh air.

A few months passed.

One day, Sara invited him for dinner. It was her best friend's pre-wedding party. Wine flowed throughout the party graciously. Sara got too drunk. Nakul felt he should drop her home. At her doorstep, she threw her arms around his neck, 'Oh, Nakul, you are such a darling,' she said, even as she reeked of liquor.

Nakul lost his composure and gave in.

The next morning, when he woke up, he felt very guilty. He had crossed a line in his marriage with Janaki. For Sara, it was not a big thing. She was not committed to anybody. While driving home, Nakul cried, 'If Janaki comes to know, what would she say?'

Fortunately, there was a message from her, 'Sorry Nakul, I missed my flight. I will come tomorrow.'

Nakul felt very relieved.

Once you cross the Lakshmana *rekha*, you lose its importance. Once you lose these moral grounds, then nothing can stop you from committing the same immoralities again because, by that time, you may get used to it.

In this vein, the casual fling between Nakul and Sara turned rather into a daily involvement, except on the weekends.

Janaki's absence was a great boon for Nakul.

Sara had started coming home and stayed the nights. Neighbours did not bother, as goes the norm in America.

As days passed, Nakul started working with more enthusiasm. Whenever Janaki was there, he would be extra nice to her, to hide his guilt. Once Janaki told Nakul, 'I have done everything but still we do not have children.'

'Don't worry Jani, we are not that old, and we still have lots of time.'

He switched the topic.

'How is your project? If it is too much for you to travel, I will travel one weekend. But see that your client is happy.'

Janaki noticed that he was different when she left. She thought that maybe her absence and distance had made him grow fonder.

It was a Tuesday. Janaki went to her office, but she felt extremely uncomfortable. She was feeling dizzy and was unable to concentrate. She sat down on a chair for some time and then she decided to visit the doctor.

The doctor examined her and asked, 'Did you do a pregnancy test?'

'No.'

'When was your last period?'

'Oh, I have totally forgotten, let me check.'

'It was seven weeks ago.'

'Maybe you are pregnant, Janaki.'

'Oh! I must inform my husband,' Janaki said, excited.

'Wait a minute. Better have a blood test to confirm, followed by a meeting with a gynaecologist.'

The gynaecologist confirmed the news.

She said, 'You are pregnant but be careful for twelve weeks. You are a little older so there are always chances of a mishap. Do not get overexcited, do not lift weights and take as much rest as possible.'

After the test was confirmed, she was on cloud nine.

She felt like telling Nakul immediately. She had received news for which they had been waiting for such a long time and felt the best way was to surprise him. That day she did not do any work. She told her client that she needed to travel that night. 'I will work this weekend, but I want two days off,' she said.

Janaki, who was highly professional, had requested time off like this for the first time. The child in her prompted her to say this.

It was a Wednesday. Nakul had assumed that there was no way that Janaki would come home. So, Sara had moved in.

But Janaki had gotten on to a plane. The whole night she did not sleep, thinking about the baby's name.

She started planning the approximate delivery time and wanted to invite her parents two weeks before that and her in-laws would arrive eight weeks after the delivery or when her parents left. In this happiness, she had pardoned her mother-in-law who was nasty to her and planned to invite them too. *After all, the child belongs to them as well*, she thought

She remembered that Uttara had sacrificed her career for the sake of her family, but she would prove that she could manage both her child and her career.

She remembered all her friends who had babies and nannies, and wanted to redesign her life now. Janaki felt the plane was moving very slowly.

By the time she reached home, it was 9 a.m. She remembered her first meeting with Nakul, years ago in Bangalore, where he had opened the door in his shorts. Janaki guessed he might look the same way today.

His car was in the portico; she knew that he always went late to the office. Quietly, she used her set of keys to open the main door. She went into the TV room and was surprised to see the dirt on the floor. There was popcorn all around the mat, beer bottles were rolling around and cigarette buds filled the ashtray.

Who could do such things? She was very upset. Janaki was a very organized person and hated an untidy house. But today she decided she would excuse Nakul for these mistakes. 'I should tell Nakul to not repeat such things and not to entertain such guests,' she said.

The staircase in the TV room led to the master bedroom on the first floor. She tiptoed upstairs and pushed open the door.

She wanted to surprise Nakul, but instead, she ended up getting surprised. Nakul was sleeping with a young girl in their bed.

Janaki understood the situation.

She screamed, 'Nakul!'

It is all she remembered before passing out from the big shock.

She lost her balance, fell to the ground and then rolled down the staircase.

Nakul was jolted out of his sleep. He too was in shock for he had never expected Janaki to come today. Secondly, he felt she would never catch him red-handed. He thought he was smart enough to manage both but had failed to do so. His 'fun-loving' adventure had destroyed his life.

Janaki was lying unconscious at the bottom of the staircase. When Nakul went to tend to her, he saw her pregnancy report and the baby and childcare book that were lying on the floor. Nakul understood the situation and started crying.

When Janaki opened her eyes, she was at the hospital. A fall from the top had resulted in a miscarriage. Nakul tried his best to explain and plead with her, but she never opened her eyes.

'Janu, I accept that I have made a big mistake. But please forgive me.'

'Janu, you are a large-hearted person, please forgive me. I will swear on anything, but please talk to me. Give me another chance.'

Nakul felt extremely guilty after finding out that he had cheated on her while she was pregnant.

He knew that it was next to impossible to repair her broken heart. Janaki would not be the same as before.

The next day, when Nakul went to the hospital, she had already been discharged. He wondered where she might have gone.

They had many friends in the city. But in this situation, she would not have gone anywhere. Nakul was concerned about how to trace her. Then there was a call from her.

'If you are free today, I will come home to pack my things.'

'Where are you calling from?'

'Holiday Inn. Later my lawyer will talk to you.'

'What?'

The phone was disconnected.

She came in the evening, packed all the important stuff and sent it to storage.

'Where are you going? I will also come with you. I want to talk to you.'

'Here onwards, only my lawyer will speak to you.'

'Janu, please.'

'Mr Nakul Apte, please don't call me that. I am Janaki Paranjape.'

Nakul knew he had reached a dead-end in his marriage.

Sumithra came to the lab earlier than she was scheduled to. She found a handsome, slightly senior person sitting in the lab and reading her book. He looked familiar but she was unable to recall where they had met.

'Good morning, Sumithra. Your book is excellent,' he said with a smile.

She felt it was a pleasant surprise but was still unable to remember.

Meantime, Prof. Keshavan came in and saw the stranger and said, 'Oh, Narayanan, when did you come? And from where?'

'I came today morning from Tokyo. But after 8 a.m., I cannot stay at home. I had to come to the Institute to meet my old friends.'

'How long are you here?' Keshavan asked.

'This time for a long period. I'm going to teach a popular science series called "Demystifying the Myths".'

Now, Sumithra remembered that he was Mr Narayanan Iyer, the celebrated astrophysicist from Berkley.

His name had been proposed for the Nobel Prize, had presented many papers in the *Nature* journal, and his book *Myths in Astronomy* was well-known. He had been working with Princeton University, and had dropped in at IISc, as he was related to Prof. Keshavan.

Sumithra was happy to see such a fun-loving, renowned scientist in her lab.

Over the next few days, Narayanan came to the Institute to deliver lectures. He preferred having his lunch only with Keshavan and Sumithra in their lab.

Narayanan had a pleasing personality that complemented his good looks. He knew when to talk, what to talk and how much to talk, which is why people were attracted to him. Apart from that, he also had a good sense of humour.

Chennai had only two seasons, a proper summer and a bearable summer. November and December were the bearable summer months. It was a long weekend. Sumithra had taken a few days off to see her family. Now, both her sisters were married and stayed in different parts of Chennai.

When she boarded the Brindavan Express, to her surprise, she saw Narayanan Iyer in the same compartment.

He said, 'Oh, it's nice to see you. Probably going home?'

'Yes, of course. What about you?'

'I have a number of relatives in Chennai; I thought I'd say hello to them,' he said with a smile.

He requested the co-passenger to exchange seats so he could sit next to Sumithra.

Narayanan knew all relatives would give him the same advice: 'You earn so much *kanna*, you are like Lord Krishna only. But you are forty years old and unmarried. I pity your mother.' Or some of them would comment: 'Do you have a white wife there in the US? Maybe that is the reason you are postponing your wedding here.'

Narayanan had been immersed in his studies ever since he was a young student. He had not bothered about marriage or anything of that sort, had a few girlfriends, but he had not talked about them at home. All those girlfriends were married to someone else now. By nature, he was a choosy person. He never wanted to marry anyone out of the community but was okay with having a short affair with anyone. He had seen how people change after marriage—couples fighting over the naming of their children and even enforcing their religions on each other.

Thus, Narayanan had developed some ideas about who he wanted to marry. He was not looking out for only a good-looking girl. He found them boring. He wanted to marry someone good-looking, intelligent and with whom he could converse.

He did like some girls. But they rejected him due to the age difference.

Then he met Sumithra.

In Chennai, it was a very pleasant coincidence that his relative's house was in the same locality as hers.

For courtesy's sake, Sumithra called him home and to her surprise, he did come. It was the first time that Sumithra had invited some man to her house. After he left, she had to answer so many questions: 'Who is he, what caste, is he married, what job, what is his birth sign, etc.'

Sumithra was about to cry and said, 'I have not planned anything, it was just a coincidence. I hardly know him.'

After she returned from Chennai, Prof. Keshavan told her, 'There is a marriage proposal for you from Mr Narayanan Iyer. What is your opinion?'

'Sir, sorry I have not thought about marriage at all.'

'No problem, take your time.'

'I need to talk to him first and then to my parents, before deciding.'

'Sure. Why not?'

That evening he came early to meet Sumithra. Slowly, he started walking from the chemistry lab to the swimming pool. As usual, in IISc the atmosphere was serene, and the route was quiet.'

Narayanan said, 'I want to ask you a few questions. If you want, you can answer. You can also ask me whatever you would like to.'

He launched his first question after a pause, 'Sumithra you are so good-looking and intelligent. Why are you still unmarried?

Sumithra took courage and told him, 'Ours is an orthodox family. My star, they say, will abruptly shorten my man's life. So, no man has come up with the courage to marry me.'

'What a foolish thing? Have you not read my book *Myths in Astronomy*? Such things are not related to each other at all. Is that the only reason? Then don't worry. I believe only in science.'

Sumithra was very happy. She had always heard compliments such as 'Sumithra you are so beautiful' or 'Sumithra you are so intelligent'. But this was the first time she had heard the word marriage attached to her name. She had never imagined this moment would come.

Narayanan said, 'I have had a few flings in the past but nothing serious. I've never dated a person with the intention of marriage. So, from my end, there is no problem. I heard a lot about you from Prof. Keshavan, and it is one of the reasons I came here. Do you have any questions for me?'

Sumithra said, 'Nothing, I'm sure I can work from anywhere in the globe.'

Just then Narayanan got a call from his home, and he said, 'Okay, I have to go now. We shall meet tomorrow.'

As soon as he reached home, he found a big drama was unfolding. Narayanan was born two months after the death of his father. His mother was a young widow and took shelter with her husband's brother and his wife. They did not have children. Narayanan grew up in their house and for all practical purposes, he was their son too.

Prof. Keshavan had informed Narayanan's family about his student, thinking they would be happy to get such a good girl like Sumithra, a renowned scientist. He assumed that they would be relieved that their son would at last be marrying a girl in the same community.

But he was totally wrong.

When he took Sumithra's name, Narayanan's aunt had a sudden recollection. As soon as Narayanan entered the house, she asked, 'Is it the same girl, daughter of Vaidyanathan and niece of Devamma?'

'The girl's father is a schoolteacher, and the girl is very good-looking,' said the mother.

'Kanna, it seems you went to her house also, without informing us.'

Narayanan thought that the grapevine in Chennai was much faster than the internet. *How on earth do these old ladies get so much information without even seeing her?* he wondered.

His uncle asked, 'It seems you both travelled on the same train?'

'How do you know all these details? Who are your informers?' Narayanan asked, surprised.

'Kanna, don't worry. We have our own network. See this is how we would be saving you from making such a grave mistake.'

'What is it?'

'You cannot marry that girl.'

'But why?'

'Because that girl's horoscope is not good. Whosoever marries her will die soon.'

'She will become just like me,' said the mother.

Narayanan's father was born with some heart disease of which he died. Everyone was aware of it, and it had nothing to do with his horoscope. However, everyone blamed Murali's birth chart.

Narayanan's aunt started, 'Kanna, you were born in the Moola star that is why you lost your father.'

'We are very modern in other ways, except when it comes to the horoscope,' his mother said.

'Kanna, when your uncle had seriously fallen ill, he survived because of my powerful horoscope,' said his aunt.

'Kanna, listen to your aunt. She has toiled her life for your sake. All of us are breathing only because of you.'

'You should marry someone with Savithri's horoscope.'

'Now who is this new girl, Savithri?' asked Narayanan.

'Ever since you have gone to America you have changed. Don't you remember the story of Satyavan Savithri. Your aunty performs a *vrat* every year to remain *sumangali* forever.'

You should marry someone who can bring back your life like Savithri brought her husband back from Yama.'

'Now don't ask who Yama is. He is the God of death.'

The ladies were crying.

Murali was dejected. Plenty of emotions unfolded.

With a sturdy voice, his mother said, 'If you marry that girl, I will eat poison at the wedding hall and die. The wedding will eventually stop.'

'Kanna, is she an *apsara*, that you are looking down upon our word?'

Without logic, his aunt started crying. His sensible uncle called him outside and said, 'Kanna, be wise and say no to that girl. Marriage should bring happiness. But this is going to be a Tamil soap opera. They will make her life miserable. Don't proceed with this union. I have lived with these two women, and I know how they are. I sincerely beg you to drop this idea. It is okay even if you remain unmarried all your life.'

Sumithra was extremely happy that night. It was for the first time that she had associated herself with love and marriage. But she was aware that she would have to adjust a lot in this marriage.

She would have to leave her present job and relocate to America. It was not an easy decision. But somewhere, somehow, you have to compromise in marriage. She had learnt this from Uttara. Sumithra dreamt of a simple marriage. Before that, she had to talk to her parents and convince them. She was sure that one of her aunts would talk to Narayanan's people about her horoscope. But this time, she felt bold because Narayanan was an astrophysicist and looked at stars more scientifically.

She dreamt the whole night. The next day, she waited for Narayanan near the swimming pool guest house and when he came, she could see that he was very sad.

Narayanan was trying to muster the courage to say what he had to. In the end, he said, 'Sumithra, please excuse me. I can't marry you.'

Sumithra stood still.

Her dreams came crashing down.

Looking at her, Narayanan repeated the same sentence.

He came near her. The unusual quietness of the streets was making Sumithra more uncomfortable.

She said, 'Keep distance.'

He firmly said, 'Sumithra, I do not have any problem. But people at home are creating a ruckus.'

'What is the use of writing a book then? If you have been unable to convince your own people at home, then how will you convince your readers?'

'As I am the only child to my parents, they don't want to take a risk.'

'What is this risk? You also believe in it, so you call it a risk and are voicing their opinion. What kind of a scientist are you? You do not walk the talk. What did you say yesterday?'

Narayanan was very upset at her remark because no one had spoken to him like that before. He asked, 'If you were in my position, what would you have done?'

'I would have married without a second thought. You have played with my feelings. I will not forgive you.'

She started walking back. Narayanan wanted to go with her as it was very dark.

'Please don't come with me. This is India. People should not think otherwise.'

She came back to her room and cried to her heart's content. She took her books from the table, put them to her heart and said, 'You are my children. I live only for you.'

When Veena, Subbu's wife, got pregnant, Diwanji's joy knew no bounds. He assigned various responsibilities to all the household staff. Now, to attend to Veena had to be each one's top priority, including Subbu's.

Poor Subbu! Diwanji had instructed him to not leave Veena's side until the child was born, whatever the reason be. And without even consulting Subbu, he cancelled all his business tours for the next eight months.

It was quite suffocating for Subbu, imagining that he had to spend his entire days with Veena till she delivered.

'Sir, how is this possible? This is common. Ladies deliver all over the world, and men need not stop working for that sake.'

'But everybody is not Veena. That means, there is no more discussion on that,' Diwanji said in a serious tone.

Subbu's family in Bangalore was also quite excited to welcome the new member of their family. Gowramma was already planning to prepare a variety of snacks and send them to her daughter-in-law, while Rajanna was evaluating to suggest to Subbu the best plan to invest in the Post Office's scheme.

Subbu's main job was to accompany Veena during her walks, her weekly medical check-ups, shopping, spa sessions etc. But he could hardly connect with her emotionally.

Gowramma and Rajanna were eager to host a baby shower for Veena, but Diwanji and Veena both disagreed saying it would strain her and that guests would pose a risk of infections. Subbu had no option but to support his wife and father-in-law.

Many times, he remembered his mother. When she was pregnant with his brother Diwakar, she had been working till the minute she went into labour. When she developed pains, her father took her to the K.C. General Hospital in an auto. She had a normal delivery and was discharged after five days. His grandmother was there to help them only for a month. Later, Gowramma resumed her work, while she tended to the baby.

But that was his experience. Now, things are different. Nearer the date, two nurses were hired round the clock and Veena's every movement was closely watched. The practical Subbu got bored towards the end of the process.

Finally, Veena delivered a baby girl.

Diwanji arranged a huge naming ceremony. Everyone who saw the baby exaggeratedly praised her, saying, 'What a great child!', 'Wow, she is so beautiful!', 'Veena was just like this when she was born', and so on. But Subbu felt that all new babies looked very cute, and their daughter was no special, except for the fact that she was Diwanji's granddaughter.

The rituals started. Subbu and Veena had to just sit through the ceremony as a formality. At the end of the ritual, the Gujarati priest called her 'Sarala'.

Subbu was utterly shocked! Sometimes, he would remember Sarala and wondered if life would have been much more meaningful had he married her. But he was trying hard to forget her very name. But now, he could not turn his back, and that name was going to be an inseparable part of his life. He asked, 'Why Sarala? Who chose this name?'

'Me,' said Diwanji, 'It is my mother's name.'

That means there is no appeal. He felt disgusted and had lost his freedom, in his own house.

Neither did Veena's friends and relatives become Subbu's friends and relatives.

Other than Lakshmi Pooja and Deepavali, there was no other celebration in the house.

He felt very lonely after marriage.

Uttara and Gopal were now in Bangalore. Arvind, who was also in the city for some work, visited them.

Uttara noticed that something was off with Arvind.

She said, 'You don't have a proper lifestyle. You eat wherever and whenever you like. This is high time that you need someone to take care of you.'

Uttara had felt sisterly affection towards him, after seeing him so unwell. She took him to the doctor, despite Arvind's protests.

The doctor confirmed that Arvind had contracted typhoid.

He had to stay in Uttara's care for the next few days, with no other choice. After all, over the years, she had become like family to him. Still, he felt obligated as he had never taken help from anyone, at any time.

'Sometime in my life, I will take help from you. So now, you don't talk,' she told Arvind when he told her that he would repay her some day.

The doctor had advised him to have two weeks' rest, but Uttara extended the care for one more week.

'Uttara, I am a goal-oriented person. A panel is coming from Delhi on a project, and I have to be there. So, please let me go,' Arvind protested.

She indeed knew the importance of his work, and without his knowledge, she had bought him a flight ticket to Haripur.

Pomela, called Pami by her close ones, was a research student at Delhi University. She was a part of a group that was going to study and make a project based on Arvind's work. So, Pami, along with her fellow research students, reached Haripur. Arvind had arranged for their food and stay. Every day, they would read, write, go around, photograph and meet people. But Pami spent more time with Arvind.

She really appreciated his work: 'We go abroad to write papers, give lectures, but we have never worked like you. You have a fundamental approach that policymakers should be decision-makers. People in this village make their own decisions, which is useful for them. It often happens that policymakers might not know the ground reality. But things here are different. I have been thinking about this for the last two weeks. I want to work with you maybe for six months. Do you mind?'

Arvind also enjoyed her company because she was so outspoken and benevolent. They had developed a healthy compatibility, and she was such a simple guest that anyone could easily afford to host her.

She had a background in theatre, and she wanted to adapt it in a way that could be used to convey many life skills to the people here. Arvind liked the idea, but he thought that the funding might not be possible for new projects. He was prepared to part with a small share of his salary.

He agreed to her request and asked her, 'You can of course continue, but what are your financial expectations?'

'Absolutely nothing. I just want to put all my experience and passion into this work. I have a scholarship grant and will use it. So, don't worry about it.'

'Do you need a certificate for your work?'

'No, I want to stay because I just want to learn many things from you. I will go back with my group, finish some paperwork and come back next month.'

Arvind nodded and was feeling good about it. He realized that if Pami returns, he would get a good resource who could add more ideas to his work.

While at Haripur, Pami would cook, sing, have fun and somehow keep things lively. Otherwise, it was such a quiet life, filled with the sounds of breeze, rain or leaves. He had very few people to talk to.

Pami returned with her group. They had spent around a month together, but in the heart of hearts, her absence had created a void in him.

She returned to Haripur within two months, this time with a computer, recorder and many such gadgets along with a moped, so that she could travel around.

Arvind had fun working with her.

Very soon, she became popular in the basti. She had her way of working—she would offer first aid to those in need, teach the children, sing and dance with them and more. It was apparent that she was enjoying her work.

Villagers started treating her like a family member. Arvind wished that someone like her would stay in Haripur forever.

He had never asked anything about her life, nor had he shared stories about himself. But Pami was smart enough. Through Prof. Parameshwaran's wife, she had found out many details about him.

One day, she asked Arvind, 'Sir, why are you not married? You have been here for a long time. You need a family of your own, and some company. Don't you think you require another pair of hands, who can work with you and make your life colourful?'

'First of all, you please stop calling me sir. Arvind is enough.

'Secondly, who will agree to come and stay here and adjust to this kind of rural life? Many people think I am wasting my time and need not have studied engineering to do this kind of job. I have accepted this lifestyle by choice and have no plans to return.'

'No, I don't agree with them. Because you are an engineer and very analytical, it does not mean that you should not do this job. You have an aim and a roadmap to follow.

'If you agree that you need someone to help you, I will stay back.'

'How long can you stay, Pami?' asked Arvind.

'Until I get married,' Pami replied, naughtily.

'Hmm. Then, you will follow your husband and again . . .' Arvind paused.

'What if my husband is also here?' Pami said. She had already set her intention.

'Great! Then all three of us can work together,' Arvind responded.

'No Arvind, only two of us will work here,' Pami said, narrowing down her words.

Arvind understood the meaning and became quiet for some time and then said, 'Are you joking?'

'No. I thought about it when I came here the last time. And I went back to Delhi for the same reason, to discuss it with my parents. My parents had long back told me that they couldn't find any man to match my mindset and had given that responsibility to me. I know there is no money here, but we will be very happy.'

'Then what about your PhD?'

'Ah! Working here is more than getting a PhD,' Pami said, not wanting to give him more time to decide.

Arvind smiled.

'Arvind, you did not even ask about my parents!'

'Sorry. But have you explained to them? Will your parents agree?'

'My parents have agreed. My father is a journalist, and my mother runs an NGO. They will be very happy to meet you.'

Arvind was happy, yet shy.

Nandita and Deonath Mukherjee were a well-known couple in Delhi's media circle. They were upright people and always fought for the right cause. Many people offered large sums to Deoji asking him to drop his writing about them or appreciate some work (that he would not have otherwise), but he refused those as he would never go against his principles. Due to his meagre salary, they were not able to afford to buy a house. And in the process, they always lived in rented houses.

Nandita very efficiently ran a school in one of Delhi's slums. Her students had done well in their life. Some of them had government jobs while a few others were abroad. They looked at her with a lot of respect and even after many years, religiously sent their contributions to her NGO. That was the only source of income for running her school. Some students who got smaller jobs and had smaller incomes volunteered for the maintenance activities. She never did any promotional or fund-raising programmes, nor did she aspire to be in the limelight. She had cultivated her identity as a no-nonsense woman.

Pomela was their only daughter. She had grown up in an atmosphere that pressed for freedom and social justice. Naturally, she was inclined toward social work. When she decided to marry Arvind, her parents were more than happy that she had found the right match. They agreed despite the age gap. They eagerly visited Haripur to meet and spend some time with Arvind.

They were very happy with his work and gave their consent.

Arvind and Pami had amicably planned their wedding and told her father, 'Baba, we don't require wedding cards. We don't want to invite many people. We just want to register our marriage. We don't need gifts from you. We are happy as we are. We will arrange a simple lunch here.'

That was perfectly fine with them. Arvind's father Chandmalji had passed away a few years ago. When the news of Arvind's marriage reached Beespur, his family was not surprised. They felt it was typical of Arvind. However, both brothers decided to at least attend the wedding and present his wife with a sari and some ornaments left behind by their mother.

Arvind sent an email to a few of his friends but other than Uttara and Gopal, no one was able to come given that it was a long commute. They had a tight schedule since their wedding was on a working day.

Subbu felt that impractical Arvind was marrying another impractical Pami. He saw no point in wasting time and money attending such a wedding.

Sumithra had teaching assignments and could not make changes to them on such short notice. She had high regard for Arvind and was in awe of Pami for agreeing to accept village life.

Sumithra could neither think of adapting to the nature of work nor could she spend more than two days at a place like Haripur.

Janaki had always been in touch with Arvind, as she would regularly send some funds for his work. However, it was not possible for her to travel only for the sake of the wedding and had promised to meet them during her next visit to India.

Uttara and Gopal arrived as they had planned.

The wedding was arranged at Arvind's house in Haripur. Warli designs, varieties of handmade *charpoy* and some wildflowers and marigold flowers were the only things that counted for decoration, but they added great charm to the simple house.

They had registered their marriage with the gram panchayat and no religious ceremony was held. Women from the same village and tribal hamlet sang folk songs. They roped in Arvind and Pami to play many folk games meant for the occasion. The feast comprised a simple vegetarian lunch prepared by the members of the tribal community. The atmosphere was very jovial.

Uttara thought back on her brother's wedding in Ramoji Film City, Hyderabad. There were more than a thousand guests that attended the many ceremonies. There was a combination of many north Indian- and south Indian-style events. The themes changed for every event, so did the outfits. Numerous gifts were exchanged. The make-up artistes stood right behind the bride and groom to give them frequent touch-ups, and the cameramen had more work, shooting them in various angles and poses as if a movie was being shot.

There were food counters abound—they had everything from starters to wine and dessert; and most of the unemptied plates were being put away.

Uttara felt she was at a huge *mela* with no purpose or joy, neither spiritual nor serene.

Arvind's wedding was a contrast, simple yet so cheerful.

After the wedding, Uttara called Arvind, and said, 'Now you are a married man. You will have one or the other expenses, at least in the first few months. Pami might not ask you, but you may have to sometimes understand. So, here, please accept this. It might come in handy any time.'

Uttara had expressed her desire to give Arvind one lakh rupees, rather than any gold or silver article, as she knew that he would not have much savings. Gopal agreed without a word. He had high regard for Uttara's empathy.

She handed over the gift to him.

Neither did she say anything more nor did Arvind. He only felt very emotional and was sure that no one else could have showered such sisterly concern, other than Uttara.

Arvind and Uttara held each other's hands, and their eyes were moist.

Years rolled by and everyone's lives changed.

Uttara had always been working, but only as a temporary or part-time faculty at whichever college closest to her house, in the city that Gopal was posted. She prioritized her family over everything. Thus, her career never took off in any real sense. She was a very affectionate daughter-in-law to Sukanya, the best companion to their children and a great support system for Gopal. Gopal always acknowledged her sacrifice. Their children were growing up and learning computers as a part of their syllabus.

One day, Uttara offered to help her son with some computer science lessons to which her daughter Malavika immediately said, 'Oh, Amma cannot teach computers. Ask Dad.'

Gopal, who was normally cool, got very upset with this and scolded Malavika, 'What do you think of your mother? She is more intelligent than me. For the sake of both of you, she has always compromised and left her career.'

Uttara tried to calm him down, but he walked out.

The children were not wrong in a way because they had never seen her true professional form, like their father's.

Once Uttara showed a college album to her children. She proudly showed off her friends.

'This is Sumithra, she has got all the awards for chemistry in India. She is a Fellow of The Royal Society'; pointing at Janaki, she said, 'This is Janaki Paranjape, who runs a huge software company in Boston and has a branch in India too. She has employed thousands of people and is one of the rare women entrepreneurs from India'; then she showed them Subba Rao and said, 'He is Subba Rao, the deputy chairman of Diwanji Company, which is very famous for textiles and more.' Showing Arvind, she said, 'We are all aware of how Arvind builds scientific toys with ordinary or recycled material. Recently, he got an award for teaching in rural India. He is transforming the tribal area.'

Her children asked, 'What about you, Amma?'

With a choked voice, Uttara said, 'I am polishing two diamonds.' Many a time she introspected, why did she not pursue her career? Was it because she was not ambitious or was it because the situation pushed her away from it? She was aware that she did not use her potential completely. Technology changes rapidly, particularly when it comes to computers, there are changes every month. Had she refrained from pursuing a career later because she had not updated her knowledge and was less confident to get back to her field? She was unable to come to a conclusion.

After divorcing Nakul, Janaki decided not to stay in Los Angeles and moved out of the city. She completely cut off ties with Nakul and immersed herself in her work.

Things changed a lot for Arvind. He was now a known face all around in his state, up to Delhi. He kept on working hard without taking any shortcuts. At Haripur too, things changed a lot.

One day, early in the morning, Rukmini knocked on Arvind's door and said, 'I think something is wrong with Param. Will you check?'

Both Arvind and Pami ran to his hut, and saw he was breathing heavily.

'Let us put him in the van. I will drive. You call the doctor,' Pami told Arvind.

The nearest hospital was eighty kilometres away. It was Sunday, still Pami managed to reach that hospital. Arvind was desperately calling doctors all the way, but no reply.

They reached the government hospital. The doctor was on leave; he had gone to the city for his personal work.

Then they rushed to a private hospital. They asked, 'Please pay the money first.'

'How much?'

'Fifty thousand.'

'Sorry, we have come in a hurry. Now we have only ten thousand. We will pay the remaining tomorrow.'

The clerk was hesitant as she had experienced bills going unpaid enough number of times. So, she was strict with the code, 'No private hospital can run on charity.'

By that time, an elderly doctor came in and recognized Arvind.

'Don't worry Mr Shah. We will admit him. I have read about you. Let us sort the other things later.'

Arvind felt happy to be recognized in time of need. Pami was very grateful to him.

They admitted Prof. Parameshwaran to the ICU. Rukmini, Pami and Arvind waited outside.

After a few hours, the doctor came out and announced that Prof. Parameshwaran had suffered a heart attack.

'He has to be stable before surgery can be performed. However, we would require more equipment and an expert. This hospital would not be able to support a procedure. You might have to go to Bhopal. But travelling in this condition is risky. Let us wait and see.'

Pami was very upset.

'I always thought working in the village was such a joy. But without a good education and medical facilities, it is so critical. No government has experts here. All of them want to stay in big cities. Even if experts manage to get a posting here, they want city life during weekends.'

She added, 'Baba had written an article about it, "The Plight of Hospitals in Villages", and today I am experiencing it.'

Arvind calmed her down and was thinking about what to do next. The best way was to go back to the government hospital to see if it had the facility and if they could catch hold of a doctor to treat Prof. Parameshwaran.

Rukmini was totally aghast and was thinking of her future, should something happen to her husband. 'My son is a heart specialist in America,' she said. 'But what is the use? His father is suffering here. Anyway, please connect me to him. I will talk once.'

Arvind connected them.

Their son was very upset upon hearing the news. 'Leaving all my appointments, it will take two days for me to reach. Give the phone to the doctor. Let me talk to him. The doctor should do the following things . . .'

The old doctor Shrivastava took the phone. Prof. Parameshwaran's son asked many questions in his American accent. He then gave instructions to Dr Shrivastava, who, being modest, heard all he had to say. In the end, he said, 'Sir we don't have the equipment which you mentioned. The patient is unstable. Until he is stable, we cannot do anything. He is under observation for the next forty-eight hours.'

This was a very critical time for all three of them, who were waiting outside the ICU. Each one was thinking in different directions.

Rukmini was in a dilemma—she did not know where she would live if her husband died. She couldn't stay here alone, she thought. She did not want to go to her children in America as she had stayed with them before and knew what it would be like.

All her brothers and sisters were old and had their own families. Even if you contribute to their income, an old lady would be considered a burden to them. Thus, she couldn't stay with them.

The only way she thought was left for her was going to an old age home. There was a place near Rajamahendri from where she hailed. She would feel comfortable with people who spoke in her mother tongue and with some relatives scattered around. She sighed and felt strange about the sudden twist in her life.

When you are young, you only look after the family, children and their education. Settling them is a big goal. But later, when the nest empties, it feels lonely. That is the reason our elders considered detachment as a good thing.

If my husband's health improves, still I don't want to stay in Haripur now, because he will need constant medical help. Maybe we should shift to an old age home which will assure medical aid, she thought. *But will he agree to move, as he is a headstrong person?* She had no answer.

Pami was thinking about a different element of the circumstance. Her father used to always talk about rural health. It is one of the most important factors why people immigrate to the city. Health expenses are also very high due to upgraded technology.

Her father once said, 'Have a medical college for every hundred kilometres and keep a feeder line for every village. Post doctors in these areas for a month, not permanently. If you post a highly qualified doctor in a village permanently, he or she will not stay. The lure of the city and private practice is so high; that will be missing in the rural hospital in pursuit of their own careers. They pressure the officials for a transfer to the city. If it is for a short period, anyone will stay. It also will not affect their family life and children's education.'

If the system had been efficiently set up today, the professor would have been admitted to a government hospital with an expert looking after him. The collapse of the health system was the root cause of misery, she thought.

Arvind had other worries on his mind. *Suppose Pami becomes pregnant, where would she deliver? When the baby is born and falls sick, where would we go?*

Arvind started thinking practically about life. All these days, he never had his own family. Now, he was worried about his unborn child and its future.

Prof. Parameswaran stabilized after two days but he had to be shifted to Bhopal. The transfer was a risky job. Arvind arranged a well-equipped ambulance for the task. The three of them escorted the ambulance in the car. Arvind thanked Dr Shrivastava for the support he had extended. This time, they carried enough money, but things did not work the way they had thought.

Prof. Parameshwaran passed away en route. It was the first realization for Arvind and Pami, of what a medical emergency meant in a village. Rukmini stayed there for some time, and as she had planned, then left for Rajamahendri.

After she left, Arvind and Pami felt very lonely. Prof. Parameshwaram and Rukmini had been like parent figures to them. The whole responsibility was now on Arvind. But fortunately, Pami was with him. Together, they improved the conditions of the tribal belt further.

Arvind started an evening school for women. After Dr Parameshwarn's death, Pami thought on medical lines. 'Arvind, I wish one of us had been a doctor. It would have helped a lot in our work.'

She had a different outlook towards things as she had travelled the country with her journalist father.

'Arvind, think over it. Between us, one should take up a political policymaking job which will help us on a larger scale. The only way to get this is through politics.'

Arvind was surprised, 'What are you saying? Neither of us is made for that.'

'It is for the benefit of the people, not for power. But you will have a say in making good policies and implementing them.

'For example, if you want to build a bridge or a hospital here, it would be easier if you are in politics. Instead of writing a hundred letters and running from pillar to post with a file, we could get permissions and construct it in the shortest time.

'You could ensure that expert doctors would work in this hospital as a part of their job. Had it been the case today, the professor would have been alive.

'You have a good reputation. People respect you. A popular person like you will win the elections because people will see what you have promised and what you have delivered.'

'I had never thought in that direction.'

'Please think. Anyway, the elections are two years away.'

A few days later, there was good news—Pami had conceived. Arvind took care that she would not deliver in this local hospital. Once bitten, twice shy.

Pami argued, 'So many women in this tribal area have delivered here. I am one of them. I don't want to leave you and go for three months. The rate of maternal mortality is very low here.'

'Pami, we do not know the future. Even if the fatalities amount to one per cent, I don't want you to be in that one per cent. I don't want to take any risk. You must deliver in Delhi.'

Reluctantly, Pami went to Delhi and came back with their son Tathagata.

Arvind soon became overprotective of his son.

Two years passed. It was time for the elections in Madhya Pradesh.

Pami pushed Arvind to contest as an independent candidate. He agreed reluctantly.

A lot of political parties rushed to Haripur.

Everyone knew that Arvind would win because of his work. They invited him to join their party. But Pami stood like a shield and did not allow anyone to poach him; she wanted him to not be affiliated to any political party.

Her parents came to Haripur during the elections. Her father pointed out, 'Arvind is contesting for a big constituency. Only a part of it is a tribal area. The remaining people will not respect him as much as tribals do, and in politics, it is just about anybody's game. So don't be overconfident.'

Arvind did not know how to canvas himself, so it was Pami who did all the promotional work. Looking at her toil, he felt she was so smart that she should have contested the elections instead of him.

Voting was over and results would be declared within two days.

It was counting day and had been raining heavily. Dulari, her helper, who looked after the house and Tathagata, hurryingly came holding a straw umbrella and asked, 'Maaji, do you have any medicine for high fever? My son has been unwell for the last two days. We have tried all our traditional medicines, but nothing is working out. I can't see him suffering. Do you have any medicine? Last time you had given him a yellow tablet and he became better.'

Pami laughed and said, 'It is an antibiotic which the doctor had prescribed. I am not a doctor and cannot prescribe any medicine. Bring your child and let us go to the doctor. He will prescribe the right medicine.'

'How to go in this rain?'

'I will take you, don't worry. But let us check if the doctor is available. The elections have just finished; he may or may not be there.'

She called the doctor, and luckily, he was there. Pami told Dulari to bring her son.

She peeped into the room and saw Arvind and Tathagata sleeping. She did not want to disturb them and quietly left.

Dulari wrapped the child in an old rug and got into the jeep. Pami called her cook Renu and said, 'You cook breakfast. I will be back soon.'

After an hour and a half, Arvind received a call. It was a surprise to him that the call was from the police who said, 'Arvind saab, your wife has had an accident. As the road was bad, the jeep skid and toppled. There were three people in the car. Another lady and child are out of danger and are in a government hospital, but your wife is stuck in the car with a head injury. Please come immediately.'

Arvind's feet became cold. He did not know what to do. He saw the moped. He told Renu and immediately left.

By the time he reached the spot, villagers were trying to get Pami out of the car. She looked helpless.

'Let us go to the hospital immediately,' shouted Arvind.

But there was no vehicle around.

'It doesn't matter. We will take her on the moped. One of you can hold her and sit.'

The pouring rain and bad roads proved to be a curse for Pami and Arvind.

Pami was murmuring, 'If only the roads were good . . . and Tathagata.'

By the time they reached the hospital, Pami had already lost a lot of blood.

She told Arvind, 'I don't think I will survive. Please see that Tathagata grows up with good values. Make good roads for others.'

'No Pami, you will not die.'

She smiled even as she bled profusely.

Pami, and with her, Arvind's inner strength, passed away.

There was a total void and Arvind went blank. He did not know how to react. Pami had come in like a breeze and went away just like one. But she had turned his life upside down. Now, he was least bothered about his election results.

He did not know what to do next. Fortunately, his parents-in-law were with him now. It was very difficult to weigh Arvind's loss against that of Pami's parents. Back home, Tathagata was crying continuously but Arvind did not have the mind space to even react. His mother-in-law mustered some strength and told Arvind, 'Look at Tathagata. You have a responsibility. Please get up and do whatever is needed now.' A few elders in the village came and helped. 'If only the roads were good'—this sentence rang in his mind day and night. He felt helpless.

The election results came out on the day of mourning. To his surprise, Arvind had lost. His very own people, for whom he had worked for more than ten years, had not voted for him due to the lure of other things. It did not make any difference to him. He felt his life was futile. The grief consumed him so much that he became very quiet.

Hearing about Pami's death, both of Arvind's brothers came down from Beespur and for the first time, he cried holding their hands.

'Munna, don't worry. We are with you,' they said. Seeing them, though they had not been in constant touch, Arvind's grief flooded out in a continuous stream. He started crying. Both brothers were very considerate. They consoled him. In the night, Ramesh said, 'Munna, look at the election results. You gave your precious life to these people. You studied so well.

If you had joined any job, you would have been in a top position now. If you had been with us, things would have been different. This is a democracy where, if somehow you get even one vote more than your opponent, you will win. This does not apply to the elections in your area, but everywhere.'

Arvind said, 'Bhaiya, if we really want to improve the lives of people, what my opponents did, is totally wrong.'

His brother said, 'Yes, that is true, but life doesn't work like that. You have seen it with your own eyes. What did you get? You stood for the elections so that you could change the situation, make good policies, better schools, roads and hospitals. In the end, the results were disastrous. You have lost your wife for no fault of hers. You lost the election, and you still want to be here? I feel, at least now you have to think practically and leave this place. Come and stay in Beespur for some time. It will be a change of scene. However, I won't be forcing you.'

'You need to understand that the equations during elections are different. There is no book on that. Politics is a complex game, it has many factors that need to be considered—power, service, ego, country's interest and also self-interest. It depends upon who stands for the elections, how they plan their position if they win and what method they choose to follow to get there. If you want to win the elections, then you should know all the factors, be prepared as if you are going to war; you should have knowledge of various types of weapons. It is left to the warrior when to use what. I'm not educated like you, but life has taught me all these lessons.'

Arvind's father-in-law encouraged the idea of a break.

'I would recommend you take a break. If you stay here, you will think of her more. Your grief will multiply. It will take some time for you to understand that she is not with you.'

He put his hand affectionately on Arvind's shoulder. His eyes were moist, and his voice was trembling. Arvind kept quiet. He was just thinking about life without Pami. He may not have felt lonely in that moment as there were people around, but once all of them left, he wondered how he would live with young Tathagata. He also asked himself for what reason he should live here. That night he thought a lot about Pami. After losing the elections she would have said, let's go away from this place or get up again and fight another election. He turned to his side and saw Tathagata sleeping beside him. The child reminded him of Pami. He thought, what kind of education and exposure will he get here? Whatever said and done, he and Pami had very good educational qualifications. What is Tathagata's future without a mother?

Arvind felt shattered in every aspect of life. Losing his mentor for not having proper medical facilities, losing his wife for not reaching the hospital on time and losing the election because of greed shown by his people—all of it made him extremely disappointed. All his idealism was slowly dissolving. His thoughts were broken by Tathagata who began crying for his mother. At that time, his older brother Suraj took charge of the situation.

'Arvind, leave all these things. Decide soon. Tathagata cannot grow up without motherly care.'

Even in that grief, Arvind said, 'No. Pami's mother will take care of Tathagata. Let him go to Delhi. But I will come to Beespur, though it's very hard for me to leave him.'

Suraj said, 'Let Tathagata study in Beespur, your *bhabhi*s will look after him. If you do not want to come, I'll take the child with me. I don't want to destroy his future.'

Arvind thought it would be better if the child lived with the grandparents. He could fill the gap of losing their own child, and he was proud of his in-laws' good values.

At last, he decided to take a break.

When he was about to leave the village, people came and pleaded with him to stay. 'Bhaiyya, don't leave. You have done so much for us and our village. It is hard for us without you,' one of them said.

Arvind did not say anything.

'Please forgive us this time. We got carried away and did not understand the consequences. Next time when you stand for elections, we will definitely vote for you,' said another.

Arvind did not respond.

Having spent several of his youthful years paying with the lives of his wife and his mentor and then losing the election, he left the place without uttering a word.

Sumithra was in Boston during her sabbatical.

A lot of things had changed in her life. Of late, she had observed that Prof. Keshavan was not happy with her. The reason was not that she had done anything wrong, but because she had become more successful than her teacher and he could not tolerate it. He always felt sad when he was introduced in any seminar as Prof. Keshavan, a good scientist and guide to Dr Sumithra. He had enjoyed being her guru and mentor, but he did not want that as his identity.

So, he had started keeping his distance from her. Initially, Sumithra did not realize. But once when she approached him for his opinion on some subject, he had said, 'Oh! You are anyway more famous than me. So why do you want my opinion!' And then, he walked out.

She was hurt but could not do anything about it and realized that success had its own enemies.

In Boston, she met Janaki. They were meeting in person after many years.

'Sumi, what is the latest news? I met Subbu. He had come to buy some software from me,' said Janaki.

She held back from saying he had only come because they were friends and so he could get a great discount which would allow him to keep the remaining money as a kickback without the company's knowledge. However, she decided to keep to her business.

She continued, 'He did not say anything much, so I also did not ask. This culture has taught me not to ask any personal questions. It is bad manners. Whereas in India, we have that freedom,' laughed Janaki.

'But still, with you, I can ask. Sumi, haven't you still met the right person?'

'In a way, no.'

For a minute, Narayanan flashed before her eyes.

'I attend Indian circles more these days. But I see that Indian girls who come here become more confident and bolder,' Janaki added.

'Why do you say that?'

'Recently a girl came for an interview. She was separated from her husband and wanted a job. By the way, you might know him. He is from your fraternity. His name is Dr Narayanan. A well-known scientist.'

'I don't know. But why did she leave him?'

'How can I ask? She had only told me that she was separated.'

Sumithra came home, and for the first time, she typed his name in Google search. She got to know that he was suffering from a disease and that he was separated from his wife.

She felt nice for a minute.

A man who believed in horoscopes must have married a girl whose horoscope had matched with his. But look how it ended.

Then she brushed her thoughts aside and said, it is fine. Everyone has a choice in life.

Arvind's brothers planned for his future with precision.

They made Arvind join the ruling party and started preparing for the elections in Beespur. The city MP was very old, so the ruling party wanted to replace him. Arvind was bright, with no background of corruption. And then, he was an engineer and had a lot of community service to his credit. He was unanimously chosen to be the best candidate to be an MP. Lots of posters were created with Arvind's quote: 'I don't want to contest for the power, but I want to contest for its policies and execution.'

Initially, Arvind felt a little agitated and disliked the propaganda, but Ramesh advised him, 'You must do this for Pami's sake. She knew that with power, you can help a lot.'

He had also learnt to speak in public. Ramesh advised, 'You should only talk about your work. Leave the asking for votes and other things to the rest of us.'

They also advised him, 'All these years, you did what you believed in and in return, you did not get anything. So, it is better that you do things that we tell you and you will see the results yourself.'

To his surprise, Arvind won the elections with a majority. He did not ask what strategy his brothers had adopted or how much they had spent, nor did they speak about it. He was made junior minister in the state.

Ramesh and Suraj were very happy that Arvind became a state minister in the very first attempt.

Though Arvind was not dishonest, he realized there were a group of people who misused his name to get favours.

Ramesh came to know this and decided, 'Every file should go through him so that he can make better decisions.'

For the first year, all the files moved automatically. The second year, Ramesh realized that he needed to take favours to go forward. One day, an old man came from Andhra and gave a suitcase to Arvind, 'Sir, this is a small gift that my boss has given for Diwali.'

Arvind was very upset. He said, 'How can you do this?'

Ramesh immediately interfered, 'Don't think my brother takes money. He does his job if the project is good.' But he took the old man to the adjacent chamber and asked for some other favour.

That very evening, Ramesh recounted the incident to Arvind, who grew further upset. 'Why did you take a favour in my name?' he asked.

'If I don't take, someone else will take in your name. This favour is not given to you because you are a good speaker, or have done social work, or are trying to bring a change or because they like you. They want a favour and that is why they are favouring you. You can do the great work that Pami had dreamt of by using your power and you need such favours to stay in this position.'

He added, 'Arvind remembered his father's words, 'When you are in an authoritative position, people respect you and once you lose, nobody cares.'

Chandmalji did not study at any university, but he knew what real life was. Thus, Arvind became the victim of a hurricane whose winds were made of dishonesty and favours.

One day, when he walked into his office, he saw Mr Parekh in the waiting room. When he saw Arvind, he stood up, bowed, and said, 'Namaste Arvindji.'

Arvind acknowledged him and went inside.

He sat for five minutes. Old memories came flooding back to him. This was the same Parekh who never offered any employee the chance to sit in front of him, even though the chairs were vacant and when youngsters were explaining their project enthusiastically, this gentleman would stop and ask about food. He was the same Parekh who used work hours for his personal tasks such as taking his wife out shopping. He felt he should not talk to him at all. But position had taught him to fake his feelings.

The best way to insult him was to not recognize him. He told the attender to call him inside. Parekh came in and bowed again with artificial obedience.

'I am Mr Parekh. I was MD at Mehta Company, when your good self was working there.'

'Oh, is it! It is long back. I don't even remember. By the way does Mr Chandmalji and his family still hold any shares in your company, Mr . . .?'

'Parekh, sir.'

Shrewd Parekh understood why he said this. Arvind had resigned for the very same reason.

'No, sir, I am not in Mehta Company now. I have my own firm. After all, your good self knows me. We want to start a small unit in your state, if you give us the licence.'

'Oh, I don't have that kind of power. I am a servant of the people. They decide who should be in politics or not,' Arvind answered tactically. He looked at his watch and Parekh understood that it was time for him to leave.

When he was almost at the door, Arvind remembered something and said, 'By the way, Mr Parekh, when your cousin was at IISc, which mess would you eat in?'

Parekh helplessly smiled and said, 'A mess, sir.'

'I always ate in B mess and also stayed in N-19. Not in M Block,' Arvind concluded.

After he left, Arvind called his brother on the intercom and asked, 'Bhaiya, take the best possible favour from Mr Parekh. I am aware of his history.'

Initially, Mr Parekh thought it would be a cake walk knowing the gullible and naïve Arvind. After talking to Ramesh, he realized it was the other way.

'I have a reason,' Arvind said and hung up the phone.

He thought how money plays an important role in society, and how he had ignored it all these days.

To have this power, one requires money, and this is a never-ending process.

When he was alone in the night, he thought of Pami. The years he had spent with her felt like a dream. Though his brothers insisted that he should marry again, he had decided not to.

He visited Tathagata as much as possible and searched for Pami's face in him.

One of Sumithra's research papers had helped the chemical industry in a very big way. Her research not only reduced the cost of a product but also increased its efficiency.

It was big news in the chemical industry. The central government decided to honour Sumithra for her contribution.

The funny thing is that the award was supposed to be handed over to Sumithra in the state where the factory was situated, to which Arvind Shah belonged.

Sumithra had flown alone to the function. All the elders at her home had passed away. She only had her parents now. Her mother was a little unwell, after spending all her best years serving the elderly without complaints. She never could live her own life. Such was the tragedy that the moment she got some freedom, she became unwell. So, her father was attending to her. Her sisters were busy with their families. Thus, no one had accompanied Sumithra.

She reached a few minutes earlier than the schedule and Arvind sent a word for her to meet him before the function.

When they sat in front of each other, they both remembered many things from the past but did not talk, as there were many other dignitaries around them. Sumithra was meeting him after a long time. Their last meeting was at Sanchi in Madhya Pradesh. He was a Gandhian then, an idealist. Today, he was a minister, widower, father to Tathagata and worldly-wise.

A lot had changed in Arvind's life, compared to everyone else in their circle. His hair had greyed, and most importantly, his innocent charm had disappeared. Arvind felt Sumithra looked more mature, almost like an elderly lady with a serious demeanour. Her beauty had faded, and her dimples disappeared.

He casually asked her, 'How are our friends?'

'You have better connection with them and know better than me.'

'Let us try to meet,' he smiled, and they walked.

While handing over the award to her, he deviated from the prepared speech. He described her as a student par excellence, extremely hard working and one who dedicated her life to the cause of science.

He added, 'No award has touched her personality, and every award has benefited with her name. It is a great pleasure and privilege to present this award to Sumithra Iyer whom I know for more than two decades.'

He wanted to invite her for dinner, but was supposed to leave for Manipur so couldn't even see her off.

Subbu woke up in the morning, looked at his palms and recited the *shloka*:

Karagre vasate Lakshmi, Karamadhye Saraswati
karamoole sada Gouri, prabhate kara darshnam

Lakshmi, the Goddess of wealth resides in the fingers of the hands, Goddess of Knowledge Saraswati, resides in the palm of the hands, the Goddess of Strength Gouri, resides at the wrist of the hands, and such hands we should see every morning.

Its actual meaning is as follows: You have to work through your hands, to get success, knowledge and strength.

The shloka was taught to him by his mother when he was two years old. He would recite it every day, in whichever part of the world he was.

Veena was having her coffee. She was quite upset because yesterday was her birthday and Subbu was supposed to come early in the evening. Unfortunately, an important client had come, and Subbu could not leave early. He reached home at midnight; Veena had waited for a long time and had fallen asleep.

How on earth could he have missed his wife's birthday, Veena could not imagine? Subbu had called her and told her that he would be late for a reason, but for her, nothing was more important than her birthday. Subbu sought her apology, 'I am extremely sorry Veena, today evening we will go out.'

Veena got upset and said, 'Today is not my birthday,' and walked out.

At times, Subbu felt, these were not important things. He felt that these rich people think they are the greatest human beings on this earth, and their celebrations are carried out all over the world. In his house, a birthday was a routine day and not much importance was given to it. Gowramma would just make payasam.

He went to the bathroom and noticed that there was a small white patch near his toe. He had not noticed it before. Then he thought he would go to the dermatologist. When he was out, Veena was packing her bag.

'Where are you going, Veena?'

'Subbu, you travel so frequently. Have I ever asked you? Then, why are you asking me?'

'I go on office work.'

'I am going on my personal work.'

Veena expressed her anger as Subbu had missed her birthday and went to her father's place. In the car, she felt ashamed. She had been preparing for her birthday for the last three months. The theme was white swan, and everyone wore white clothes. Pictures of swans were placed all around the room. The cake was swan-shaped, and the cutting knife was white. They all waited for Subbu for twenty minutes and then cut the cake. She felt everybody had been laughing at her.

'Oh Veena, what a workaholic husband you have! Your husband does not know about work–life balance.' These words echoed through her ears.

Tears rolled down her cheeks, and she thought she must tell her father to intervene and advise Subbu to give some attention to her.

Neither Subbu nor Veena were dependent on each other. They had cooks and separate drivers. The following day, Subbu completed his work in the evening and remembered that he had to meet the dermatologist. He had his own doctor, away from Diwanji's personal physician. By this time, he knew the trick of the trade, what had to be common and what should not. Most of the things were uncommon and hidden. When he went to his doctor and casually showed him the white spot, he thought the doctor would give some ointment and tell him to apply for a few weeks. But the doctor did not do that. They started examining the patch, asked for blood test and even pricked the area.

After the examination was over, he asked the doctor what it was.

'Relax Mr Rao, this looks like a small patch affected by leprosy.'

Subbu was stunned. He was unable to wear his shoes and sat motionless. The doctor expected that and continued, 'Mr Rao, you don't have to worry. This is curable. It is not contagious. If you take medicine properly, then you will be fine. In olden days, there was no cure for this and hence, people got scared. But now, modern medicine has found a solution for this.'

'How long do I have to take treatment, Doctor?' Subbu asked in a hushed tone.

'Depends from person to person. Normally, for three to four or six to eight years.'

Subbu was lost in himself and requested the doctor to keep this confidential. Once he was in the car, he felt like he was going to burst out but then he was conscious of the driver's presence. Neither did he have any genuine friend with whom he could share, nor could he say this to a family member. He always made friends where he would have an advantage. He was friendly with Janaki, Sumithra and Gopal, much less with Uttara and absolutely not with Arvind.

He remembered that long back Arvind had invited him to see his work at Haripur, but he had dismissed it thinking there was nothing here for him. He looked at it as a useless job and opined that all people who were doing philanthropy had no ambitions.

'What will you get if you make someone happy? You should look after yourself and make yourself happy,' was his motto.

Once Arvind had written to him saying that he required a few borewells in his village. He had asked if Subbu could do it as a part of their corporate social responsibility activity.

Subbu had felt he would be wasting money by funding that project.

If I help to set up a borewell in that area, no one will recognize it and no one will ever come to know that I have paid for it; what money I spend should give me visibility or some benefit, he had thought.

Haripur did not fit in with his strategy. Instead, he felt that if he did anything in Mumbai, he could invite a minister, put a nameplate on that as 'donated by' and encash his philanthropy.

He had not even replied to Arvind's email. Furthermore, he had always looked down upon Uttara, because with her intelligence, she could have made lots of money. Instead of that, she had landed jobs as a temporary lecturer. He always felt Uttara should have married an affluent person from Hyderabad and managed her career by helping her father.

For Subbu, Janaki was the best. She had her own company and made good money.

Neither could he share his current situation with his mother, as she was orthodox and could not understand modern medical science, nor could he share it with Veena, as her reaction would be entirely different.

As he was brought up in a conservative manner, he wondered if this was due to a curse from Sarala.

Then his scientific temperament said that one could not get a disease from a curse. It can happen to any human being. This kind of thinking suited people who lived thousands of years ago.

His anxious mind settled down after some time. He was sure that medicines would help him more than anything else. But he was thinking how to hide this from Veena.

His doctors advised him to take treatment from a leprosy specialist.

'In that case, I do not want a doctor from Mumbai. Can you suggest any good doctor outside of Mumbai, in a city that is connected by flight? So that nobody finds out?' he had told his doctor.

The doctor had thought for a minute and said, 'Yes, I know Dr Sambashivan in Chennai. He is one of the most ethical doctors. You can go there.'

Now, Subbu started wearing socks at home. Initially, Veena did not bother. However, when Veena saw him wearing those in summer, she became curious and questioned him. 'Oh, my feet are feeling cold. That is all. Don't worry. I am perfectly fine.'

Then, he thought for a minute and continued, 'I will shift to another room so that I can use the AC on and off. You can be comfortable here.'

Veena agreed immediately.

Subbu was relieved that he could sleep without socks, because they were also uncomfortable for him.

After a few days, when he was walking out of Dr Sambashivan's clinic, he saw Uttara there. She was going inside the clinic in a hurry, but he waited for her to return. He felt nice that someone whom he knew was also going through similar agony. He was relieved thinking that it was quite a common disease, and that only he was unaware of it.

He felt like a lonely traveller looking for a co-traveler in a desert. When Uttara came out, they were pleasantly surprised to see each other. Subbu greeted her and said, 'Let us talk for some time, unless you are in a hurry.'

'Sure, let us go. I am not in a hurry,' said Uttara.

They settled in a lounge. Subbu started talking, 'It was so sudden that I did not realize how this happened to me. Initially I was so scared. Now I feel much better. What about you, Uttara? Don't get scared; it is curable.'

Uttara did not talk. After some time, she said, 'No Subbu, I am here for some other reason.'

Subbu felt he was caught red-handed, and he had spilled the beans himself. Unknowingly, he had shared the most secret news with his friend.

'Then why did you come here?' Subbu asked her.

'During my free time, I work with leprosy patients in Bangalore. So, I came to invite the doctor for a lecture.'

'Uttara, don't tell this to anyone please.'

'No Subbu, I am not a person like that. I will die with this news. I work in this area, and I know the mental agony of the patient. But it is completely curable, and I have seen that with a lot of people. In olden days, people would get scared of tuberculosis; but now, no one bothers because there is treatment and complete cure. Have courage.'

She placed her hands on Subbu's hands with affection and then, she left.

A few words from Uttara made him feel relaxed and now, he felt that it would be good to have a friend around. They were useful in difficult times.

Prof. Keshavan called Uttara for his son's housewarming ceremony in an apartment built by Dinshaw Company, which was very well known for its quality work.

Uttara, who kept in touch with everyone, was surprised upon noticing Sumithra's absence.

Unknowingly Uttara asked, 'Sir, where is Sumithra? How is she?'

'You are her friend, and you should know better about her whereabouts. Most of the time, she is abroad. Sumithra's story is like Michael Faraday's. Sir Davy was a well-known scientist and Michael Faraday was his assistant. But till now, everybody says that the greatest discovery of Sir Davy was Michael Farady. Similarly, that is how I am known to others today,' Prof. Keshavan said in a sarcastic tone.

Uttara had taken both her kids to Delhi to show them the Republic Day parade. She wanted to meet Arvind who was also there for the parade, but Gopal had said, 'Let us not disturb him. He is a big man now and a busy person.'

'For me it does not matter what he is; we are good old friends. We will just try. If he is free, we shall meet, else I am fine,' Uttara said naïvely.

Arvind was discussing his travel plan for some election. The phone rang and his personal assistant, Mr David, said that he was very busy.

'That is fine. Just leave a message that Uttara Rao had called him,' Uttara said.

David wrote the name, spelling it loudly as he did. It alerted Arvind. He said, 'Wait a minute. What name did you say?'

'Uttara Rao.'

Immediately, he took the phone, and to everybody's surprise, he spoke, 'Hi Uttara, where are you calling from?'

'From, Hotel Ashoka.'

'Have you come with your children?'

'Yes.'

'Okay. I will send the car. We shall meet up for dinner at my place. I will call Tathagata also. Give your details to my personal assistant.'

He handed over the phone to David.

That evening, when Arvind was returning home, he remembered many things about Uttara—her affection, the way she had nursed him when he had typhoid, when she had visited him at his wedding and the way she had consoled him after Pami's death. *This is what a real sister would be like*, he thought. She had retained her genuine nature through ups and downs of life, which was rare.

The children had lots of fun at his house. Arvind forgot his position and age. He became like a schoolteacher once again.

He told Uttara, 'As long as you are here, don't hire a car. You can use mine. I am also arranging a pass for the parade. You are my personal guest.'

Then he went inside, searched for something and gave it to her children. 'Uttara, it is not meant for you, it is only for your children,' he joked.

When they went home and opened the present, there were scientific puzzles inside the packaging and a children's book written by him and Pami, when they were at Haripur.

Uttara had tears in her eyes, remembering Pami.

Veena wanted Sarala to join the Wellington School in Dehradun, which is supposed to be one of the best boarding schools for girls. Veena had also studied there, which is why she wanted Sarala to go there.

But as there were too many applications, the school authorities had requested the shortlisted candidates to complete the admission process as soon as they announced the first list.

That day, Veena received a mail that Sarala had been admitted to the school and the formalities had to be completed the same day. Veena was overwhelmed and wanted Subbu's signature on the admission form.

She went to Subbu's room.

Subbu was sitting on his chair and applying ointment to his foot. Veena stopped for a minute and asked, 'What is this white patch, Subbu?'

Before Subbu could answer, she asked, 'Is it leukoderma? I am scared of it.'

Veena stepped back.

Subbu was quiet, thinking what he should say.

'Which doctor are you going to? Is it hereditary? Contagious? Is that the reason you are wearing socks all the time? That is why you are sleeping separately.'

Subbu knew that she would not leave the topic and would want to talk to the doctor, and it was best to tell her everything.

Calmly he said, 'It is not leukoderma. It is leprosy, and it is curable. It is not contagious. I am taking treatment.'

'Why did you not tell me this before?'

He remained silent.

She went out of the room and returned after half an hour to the dining table.

'I thought about it. Now, let us live like two strangers in this house. I will not tell this to Daddy. At this age, I don't want to trouble him. Fortunately, Sarala is going to a hostel, and I don't want to share anything with you. We will have our own separate paths and lives.'

After Janaki left Nakul, he became very lonely. He regretted his actions a lot. Sara finished her internship and went away. He continued his job with IBM. His parents felt he should marry again, but he was not prepared.

He was now due to be promoted as the vice president of the company, and he had tough competition for it. All the candidates were equally good.

His boss had played the card very well.

'Nakul, if you want to be the next VP, then you must prove that you are better than others. You have pitched to Google for software. It is a very important project. You go to San Francisco and bring the contract. If you do that, probably you will be the VP of this company. Your incentives and perks will be very high. Think over it, but only if you bring that contract.'

Nakul felt that he must do this job, work hard, get all the data ready as well as practise his presentation. He remembered how, in the Mahabharata, Arjuna saw only the eyes of the bird in his bow-and-arrow test; he thought he should have a similar focus. But poor

Arjun forgot that there was equally good Karna on the other side.

When he got down and was waiting for his luggage at San Francisco, to his surprise, he saw Janaki. She was also waiting for her luggage, but she had not seen him.

Janaki was not just his ex-wife. She was the one who had taken him to America and helped him set up his career, shared a few years of her life with him.

He himself went and talked to her, 'Hello, Janaki.'

She turned back and without any emotion said, 'Hi, Nakul.'

'What brings you here, Janaki?'

'My work.'

Her luggage arrived by that time. She picked it up and walked away.

Nakul felt sad. He thought she should have spoken a few more words, at least for courtesy's sake.

She talked less than normal. He had lost the relationship with her.

His presentation was scheduled for 10 a.m. the next day. He did very well and could make out that the panel was also impressed. With great confidence he asked them, 'When will I know the results?'

'We will let you know by email,' they said.

He stepped out of the room confidently, but within a minute, he stood like a statue. The next person entering the interview was Janaki Paranjape. He was worried that Janaki would outdo him and bag the contract.

Another thought crossed his mind. *She might be intelligent, but sales-wise I am better than her. After all, I am a marketing graduate from Stanford. She might be a good researcher, but she was a very straightforward person, who can never do sales talk of diplomacy. She might not even be in the race.*

Janaki had once told him, 'The best sales strategy is to tell the client both positive and negative of your product. Be transparent with your client. There should not be surprises. No product is perfect. But when you tell the drawbacks, you are establishing reliability with your clients. Leave the final decision to them, but don't push it. If you work with these principles, you will get repeated orders.'

Nakul had never believed in this strategy.

He felt lazy at the hotel and decided to hit the bar on the premises. As soon as he reached there, he received the email from the officials who had seen his presentation.

'Your presentation was excellent. We are happy about it. But due to a set of constraints, we are unable to work with you. However, if the first contender declines, you will be joining us. Wish you all the best.'

Nakul was very upset, as though he was caught in a whirlwind, unaware. Arjuna had lost his bet. He always had thought he was the best, but he had forgotten that the son of Radha had defeated him effortlessly.

He did not know what to say to his bosses. He knew that it was Janaki who had defeated him in his own game.

If he had lost to someone else, he would have probably accepted it and not felt bad. But losing to Janaki was unbearable. He ordered more drinks and sat in a gloomy corner. Around 10 in the night, he was exhausted, but he was awake and felt someone gently touching his shoulder.

He turned back and saw the person.

His failure, his anger, flared up.

'Congratulations, Janaki Paranjape, I think you planned to come here only to see my defeat.'

She came in front of him and sat on another chair. 'No, I have come here to talk to you as a friend.'

'All lies. You are here only to put me down.'

'If I knew that you were coming, I would not have come,' she said.

Nakul started arguing with her. 'It may make you very happy to know that I will not become the vice president; you stole my honour.'

'Yes, I know.'

'But how do you know this condition put on me by my company?'

'Because we are in the same business. There is nothing confidential.'

'What promotion are you getting from this contract?'

Normally, a drunk person talks only about what is on his mind, without any filter.

'I have my own company. Hence, I do not require any promotion. However, I just wanted to tell you that I have declined this.'

'What?' Nakul said, surprised. His intoxication subsided.

'I just wanted to try among the big IT giants. I wanted to know what the role of a small company like ours would be? Could we do it?'

'With this contract, you would have got a lot of money and contracts. Why do you want to leave?'

'I would not have left it for anybody else. I will leave only for your sake. I am all alone. I don't have any desire. I like my job, and I do it well. I enjoy being an entrepreneur. Whereas your life is dependent on it.'

Nakul could not believe it. He knew that Janaki would never lie or talk to please somebody. She would never talk behind anybody's back and played absolutely no politics.

He looked at her. She was sobbing.

It was very unusual of her. He had seen many facades of Janaki—the tennis champion, the efficient Janaki, the hardworking and the bold.

Nakul softened. He caught both her hands and said, 'Janaki, please forgive me. Let us not live in this country. This country reminds us of many unwanted incidents. We will start a fresh life!'

'No, Nakul. I understand you and your feelings. We have walked separately in our journey for a long time now. I have lost trust in marriage. I have only one request. If possible, let's try to never meet again.'

Uttara and Gopal settled in Bangalore. They built their own house. One day, Gopal came home and was very quiet. Uttara realized that there was something wrong, but she allowed him to settle down.

After some time, she asked, 'Are you fine, Gopal?'

'There is something wrong with Arvind. Some day, that will create a havoc in his career.'

'What has happened?'

'We lost the contract.'

'It is business. Sometimes you win and sometimes you lose. It is a part of the game. And in what way is Arvind connected?'

'I am not worried about losing the contract. I am worried about the way we lost it, and Arvind had a hand in that.'

'What are you saying?' Uttara was a little taken aback.

'We applied for the licence, and we came to know that Arvind wants favours to sign this paper. And I specifically told our people not to give it, because we had all the documents in place. Just because we did not meet their demands, we lost it.'

'Did Arvind know that it is yours?'

'Of course, he knew. But still, he did it. I do not know his obligations or pressures. I felt sorry for Arvind, because a man of principles, a true Gandhian, a great social worker, has changed with power. That hurts me more than losing the contract.'

'Do you think I should speak with him? He does listen to me.'

'No. He is riding a tiger. He cannot get down. He is an adult and knows what he is doing. You can only pray that he should not get trapped in any trouble anytime in his life.'

'Did the other vendor accept his conditions?'

'Of course, they have always done so, because they always deviate.'

'Who are those people?'

'S.V. Constructions, Hyderabad.'

Now, Sumithra was back in India and Uttara wanted to visit her.

It was after many years that Uttara was about to visit Indian Institute of Science. She felt life was like a flowing river and everyone was like a piece of wood floating on it. They may join at one place and disjoin at the other. She remembered Subbu, Janaki and Arvind.

So many people get married inspite of all odds. But why did our Sumi not marry at all? Did she never meet any man according to her taste? Or did she feel she was more attracted to chemistry?

When Uttara looked at the old building of the college, lecture hall and library, nothing had changed. They all remained the same. Then she looked at the lecture hall complex L-11. This was the place where she had first met Gopal. She smiled to herself.

Uttara looked at the beautiful green meadow and remembered their romance. She went to the Computer Centre and remembered the old bet: 'Heads I win, tail you lose.'

She remembered her classmates and went towards the ladies' hostel; she reminisced on the green-eyed

Janaki, the beautiful Sumithra, the thin and tall Arvind and handsome Subbu in N-19.

'I wish those days would come back,' she said.

Sumithra was giving a lecture, and Uttara was waiting for her to finish.

Sumithra came out and they both were happy looking at each other and hugged.

'I think we have put on weight,' Uttara said.

'Yes, we are nearing fifty,' Sumithra said, and smiled.

'Do you remember Sumi, Arvind used to call you *mimosa pudica*.'

'Yes, I was very shy. He used to call me touch-me-not. Now, I am bold. Nothing scares me!'

'Sumi, how is the Institute now?'

'Oh, it has changed a lot. Now, girls hardly wear any sari or salwar kameez. Computers have also changed. Every department has a computer centre now. We used to think that email was a new invention. Today, unless it is official, there are many other applications. Everyone is tech savvy.'

'Hey Sumi, shall we eat at the mess?'

'Sure, but you will not enjoy the food now.'

On her way, some people were pointing at her and saying, 'She is Sumithra madam, who has received the honour of Fellow of Royal Society.'

Ye daulat bhi lelo, ye shaurat bhi lelo
Bhale cheenalo mujse meri jawani
Magar mujko lautado bachpan ka sawan
Woh kagaz ka kashti
Woh baarish ka paani

—Lyricis by Sudarshan Fakir, music
by Jagjit and Chitra Singh

Uttara had connected with everyone through WhatsApp and conveyed the date, time and venue of their promised reunion.

It was exactly after twenty-five years, and at the same place—under the neem tree at the Institute from where they had gone their separate ways. Arvind saw the WhatsApp message and told his secretary David, 'I want to go to Bangalore for two days. It is my personal travel. So don't schedule anything. I don't need a hotel or car. I will arrange everything myself.'

He recalled a few memories—his maiden railway journey, going to Hyderabad to Uttara's home, meeting

Sumithra for the first time in the night and how Subbu had hidden the book that he needed for the test. He remembered that he had asked for a borewell when he was in Haripur, and Subbu had not even replied.

When he became minister, Subbu had come to meet him with a big bouquet. Despite knowing his intention, Arvind had still talked to him. He remembered Pami. If she had been alive today, he didn't know whether he would have been a minister or not. But, she would have been able to meet all his friends.

Twenty-five years had changed so much in him. He was at a juncture which he had never imagined. Everyone remained more or less in their own field, except him. He had deviated so much from the ideals, subject and vision.

What an irony of life!

Subbu called Uttara and told her that he might not come because everyone would ask about Veena, and he would be unable to answer.

'Nobody will ask. This is our meeting, not our spouses,' she had said. 'Even if they ask, tell them Veena has gone to Dehradun for a PTA. I will support you. But please do come. I do not know where we will be after the next twenty-five years. Let us not give reasons and waste our precious time. By the way, how are you?'

'I am improving, thank you. Okay then, see you in Bangalore.'

For Sumithra, it was very easy. She was already at the Institute and was available anytime.

Janaki made a special trip. She planned to first stop in Bangalore and then visit her parents in Pune.

Gopal, who was the witness, had also planned to come.

There were dark clouds, but it was not raining. New students were settling in at IISc. Some of them came from distant places. They were all standing in a queue for admission.

Sumithra, who was the last one to join the Institute among her friends, was the first to come in for the reunion. Arvind took a drop till the Institute gate and walked inside. Upon seeing him, some people whispered, 'Why is Arvind Shah here? Is there any function today?' They were unaware of Arvind's ways of working. Subbu came from Chennai. After the meeting, he planned to meet his mother and return to Mumbai the next day. But nowadays, he prefered to stay at the Windsor Manor than with his brother and parents.

Janaki came from the Westend, though Uttara wanted her to stay with her.

There were also whispers when Janaki walked in. 'Oh, she is the famous entrepreneur Janaki Paranjape.'

The least recognized person was Uttara.

Uttara said, 'Look how everyone is talking about how successful you are, Janaki.'

'What is success, Uttara?'

'Overall, I might look very successful but am actually not,' said Janaki.

'But why? You are doing so well,' said Sumithra.

'I lost my career. Sumi, you are among the most successful here,' said Uttara.

'Yes, only in chemistry. But my other dreams are unfulfilled.'

Janaki aimed at Subbu now, 'Subbu you are the best one. You have realized your dreams.'

At what cost? Subbu thought. He then said to Janaki, 'I don't know. But I think Arvind is the most successful one here.'

'Then I am the best actor,' said Arvind.

Everyone laughed.

'I am not at all successful,' said Uttara.

'Why, you have an excellent husband, good family life, good children, what else do you want?' said Arvind.

Gopal summoned up, 'It is very difficult to sum up success from someone else's view. It is like four blind men and an elephant. Everybody defines success the way they want, and they measure someone else's life with that yardstick. There is no complete success or complete failure. What brings happiness to us internally is success and can be measured with your own yardstick.'

Everybody agreed.

'When shall we meet again?'

'We are all growing old, let's meet as much as possible. We have to try to remain connected.'

'Let us stay in touch as much as possible,' said Uttara.

'Shall we have lunch in the Institute's mess, on Sumithra's account? She is the only one who can get us in now,' said Uttara.

'No, I can't. I am taking Ayurvedic treatment for my blood pressure,' said Subbu

'Oh, I am not used to having lunch in the afternoons. I have ten cups of tea a day,' said Arvind.

'I am on a keto diet. So, I can't eat,' said Janaki.

'We are not worried about our weight. So, we will eat,' said Sumithra and Uttara.

Everyone laughed loudly and started walking to the mess.

Scan QR code to access the
Penguin Random House India website